Also by Brenda Hasse

<u>An afterlife journey Series</u>

On The Third Day

<u>Young Adult</u>

The Freelancer

A Lady's Destiny

Wilkinshire

<u>Children</u>

My Horsy And Me, What Can We Be?

Yes, I Am Loved

A Unicorn For My Birthday

From Beyond The Grave

~

Brenda Hasse

From Beyond The Grave

ISBN: 978-0-9906312-7-9 (pbk)

ISBN: 978-0-9906312=8-6 (ebk)

To Mrs. B., my neighbor.

Mom's Funeral

My attention was drawn to a circle of light that appeared on the church floor in front of Mom's casket. My eyes traced the sparkling dust particles upward to a wooden beam in the vaulted ceiling. It didn't make any sense. How could a beam of light pass through the ceiling? A calmness settled deep within me, alleviating any fear. In fact, I found it comforting.

I clutched Dad's arm, leaned toward him, and whispered, "Look." I pointed to the light on the floor, but he raised his shoulders and shook his head, indicating he didn't understand. I persisted by pointing my finger toward the strange phenomenon coming from the wooden beam, but it disappeared as he looked toward the ceiling.

Even though the past few days had been stressful, I was certain I hadn't imagined what I'd seen. But as self-doubt crept into my mind, I wondered if the hallucination was caused by the grief and exhaustion I was experiencing.

As the congregation replied "Amen," my mind snapped back to the reality of the situation. The priest droned on, everyone went through the routine 'church aerobics,' and we took our leisurely lap to receive communion.

Like most people my age, I did not enjoy attending Mass. It was the same old boring service, except for the readings that changed weekly. During the hour and fifteen minutes of weekly obligation, the highlight was watching people pass by my pew on their way to receive communion. I often saw familiar faces and would smile at fellow classmates who returned a subtle nod or wave indicating they had seen me as well.

But today I really did not want to see anyone. I kept my head down.

With a final blessing from the priest, the Mass ended. We followed Mom's casket out of the church, stood nearby as the pallbearers loaded it into the back of the white hearse, and went to our powder blue limo provided by the funeral home.

Hearing the hearse door close, I paused to see Mom's body safely inside. I glanced in the direction of the cemetery, a short distance away. Someday, Dad would be joining her in his adjacent plot. I prayed he would not join her for many years yet.

FROM BEYOND THE GRAVE

I knew it sounded selfish of me to say so, but I needed him in my life, if for nothing else than stability.

I had a lot of big things coming up; graduation, college, and hopefully, someday, marriage. I wanted him there to walk me down the aisle.

I imagined my wedding would be the most difficult milestone in my life to get through without Mom. As if she had anticipated her death, it was an event we had talked about often. We had exchanged ideas, and planned the preliminaries, even though it was premature. I didn't even have a boyfriend. There were times I felt left out, an outsider at school because my friends did, but Mom always insisted I focus on myself. Her sound advice still echoed within my mind.

"There is plenty of time for you to have a man in your life, later down the road, after high school. For now, you need to focus on yourself. This is your time. One day some good-looking guy will stand back, look past your beauty, and notice the ambition, confidence, and intelligence you possess, and admire those attributes. Then you must decide if he is right for you. But beware. Sometimes men are attracted to such a woman because they are lazy, and they would just as soon have you take care of them. In truth, that type of person is more like a child and you would be fulfilling the role of their mother. You want to be selective. Don't be blinded by love. Examine each suitor's attributes and qualities and ask yourself if you can tolerate their personality for a lifetime. Until that time comes, focus on yourself and what you want to accomplish. When the average age of marriage for a guy is 27 years old, do you think a 17 or 18-year old guy is serious about a relationship?"

She had a point. It seemed as if couples in my class who hooked up for prom soon separated afterward. For those still going steady, I could only assume the same would happen to them if they attended different universities after graduation.

I took her advice to heart and focused on my studies and sports. I made a habit of 'just being friends' with guys who expressed an interest in wanting more than that. In truth, with Mom's illness, I had little time for them. God, I missed her already. How was I going to get through my life without her there, without her advice? She was my best friend.

Dad held the hearse door open as he waited.

"Get in the car, honey."

Pulled from my thoughts, I glanced at him before looking to the white hearse with its doors closed and the driver waiting inside.

After seating myself in the back seat of the limo, I looked at the orange flags on each side of the hood of the car waving in the breeze as if they were bidding farewell. I was joined by my younger brother and Dad before our car followed the hearse to the cemetery. I turned and looked out the rear window. The parade of cars with their headlights shining brightly and waving orange flags was long. Turning back, we were silent as we traveled the short drive to the cemetery.

FROM BEYOND THE GRAVE

We passed through the ornate archway of the entrance. The solemn procession crept to a standstill on the blacktop pathway adjacent to where the readied plot waited. It had green indoor/outdoor carpeting around the edges of the rectangle hole. A small canopy tent had been erected to shade us from the sun, with chairs overlooking where Mom's body would be placed for eternity.

We waited in the car for several minutes as the guests parked their vehicles and gathered around the site. Mom's casket was guided out of the hearse. The funeral director adjusted the rose bouquet on the top of the casket before it was carried by the pallbearers to the grave. One of the funeral assistants opened our car door, and we emerged and followed the casket. The funeral director indicated for us to sit in the appointed chairs reserved for family. He handed each of us a pink rose, and the priest began speaking. I wasn't in the mood to listen.

Poems were read and white homing pigeons were released. The priest motioned for us to rise. I took a deep, cleansing breath as I stood from my seat, my heart racing, hoping to keep my tears in check. We stepped forward and placed each rose on the casket before watching numbly as it was lowered into the ground. Dad used a small chrome shovel to take a bit of dirt and drop it onto the casket lid. A few last words were spoken by the priest. Something about the reception in celebration of life to follow.

We returned to our car and were driven back to the church hall. Some of the attending guests followed while others went home.

I'm not certain which church committee was responsible, but the tables were dressed in lovely linen tablecloths with flower centerpieces. The food was served buffet style and looked quite delicious. I helped myself to some pasta and salad.

I sat with my brother and Dad at our usual coffee and donuts table. It was strange to see Mom's chair empty. Our uncle, who I seldom saw and the only member of Dad's family in attendance, sat next to Dad. I was quite surprised when Grandma joined us. Maybe she thought our table was reserved for family.

I pushed my food around my plate with my fork. Even though the food was tasty, I had little appetite.

Dad ate quickly, excused himself, and left to visit with guests seated at other tables. Grandma did so as well.

As the afternoon dragged on, it seemed as if no one wanted to leave, quite opposite of my desire. Many paused at our table on their way out of the hall to express their condolences. I forced a smile upon my face, remained tightlipped, or replied with only a word or two.

My brother leaned toward me and spoke for my ears only.

"I'm ready to go. How about you?"

I sighed as I looked to the remaining guests.

"Yes, but I know we can't go until everyone has left."

The funeral director entered the hall and handed Dad his keys. He had kindly brought his car from the funeral home to the church hall. Dad expressed his gratitude for all he and his staff had done for us over the past few days.

The last of the guests accompanied us out of the hall. After the short drive home, stepping over the threshold of our house seemed strange. I let out a sigh, inhaled Mom's lingering perfume, and wiped a tear from my cheek. I wanted to put the day behind me, thankful the final goodbye was over.

I went to the kitchen, took a cookie from the cookie jar, and entered the living room where Mom's desk sat empty. So many times I had entered the room to see paperwork piled high on her desk. She would look over the top of her reading glasses and ask what I wanted. I put the remainder of the cookie in my mouth as I stopped before her desk and stared at the white feather lying on the protective glass top. I picked it up, twirled it between my thumb and index finger. *Strange. Is this a feather from your angel wings, Mom?*

I went to my room to change into something more comfortable and took the feather with me.

On The Other Side

Old Bill nodded his head bidding me farewell. He turned and left with his spirit guide. His faithful dog, Brutus, followed.

As I looked around the brightly lit chamber, I sighed. Crossing over had been painless and easier than I'd thought. I had simply relaxed and let it happen. In all honesty, I'd had little choice in the matter. But now that I was dead, I found myself idle and wondering. I looked to my steadfast spirit guide.

"Now what?"

"*All will be revealed.*" My spirit guide continued to communicate with me telepathically. He closed his eyes.

Details of my past lives flooded my mind, as if a curtain had been opened to reveal the knowledge. Over a hundred lives extending as far back as Lemuria, Atlantis, and the building of the central pyramid in Egypt. I grinned knowing many believed some of the cities to be fictional. I knew each purpose of every life. Yes, I was royalty, of Stewart blood, and had been a lady in waiting for Mary, Queen of Scots. I had lived both sexes, male and female, with each life responsible for teaching and/or learning. Some of my lives were surrounded by luxury, others by poverty. Some I was athletic, others quite stout. Every question was answered. The hidden knowledge became crystal clear. I watched as my guide opened his eyes as he finished the task.

"*Now that all has been revealed, you may ready yourself for your next life.*"

"My next life? So soon?"

"*As soon as you are ready. But first, your purpose must be determined.*"

"You mean, what I'm to learn or teach."

My spirit guided nodded in acknowledgment.

"How soon do most people wait before beginning another life?"

"*It depends on the soul. For those who believe in the afterlife, their transition to the next life is easy and may happen immediately upon the death of their previous life. In fact, some are quite eager to begin their next life. For those who do not believe in the afterlife, they must be re-educated. Unfortunately, for the stubborn minded, it takes a long time. Since you are a believer, you may begin your next life now."*

"So, I have got a lot yet to learn?"

"You will live as many lives as necessary in order to learn all you must know. If for any reason you fail to learn an assigned lesson, the lesson will be reassigned to you during your next life. It is normal to live between one hundred to two hundred lives."

"And when we learn all we must learn, then what?"

"The choice may be made to become a spirit guide, a teacher, or remain here. If you are not ready to begin your next life, you may choose to retain what has been revealed to you, remain in your spirit form, and delay your next life until you are ready."

I toured the room, which was spacious, bright, almost glowing, and filled with love.

"How is my family doing?"

"They grieve, but they are doing as well as to be expected."

"I see."

"You may be pleased to know that your daughter found the feather you left on the desk. She has kept it."

"I miss her. We were very close."

"She is an old soul."

"In truth, I miss all of them."

"You may see them any time you wish."

I turned to face my spirit guide. His revelation caught me by surprise.

"How? For how long?"

"*You may stay with them for short periods, throughout the remainder of their life, and be present when they complete their purpose.*"

"You mean when they die?"

"Yes."

Moving Forward

I lay in bed, half awake, reluctant to begin my day. To alert me that it was past his normal feeding time, Spooky scooted a book across my dresser until it fell on the floor. I kept my eyes closed, pretending to be asleep. He knew I was awake. My hairbrush was next to fall to the floor, then my bottle of hand lotion.

"Enough, Spooky."

Mission accomplished. Spooky jumped on my bed, walked on my pillow circling my head, and touched his damp nose to my cheek. I opened my eyes, pushed him aside, and looked through my bedroom window at the bright sunshine of the morning. It was Sunday, a day Dad usually woke us to attend church. The time on my alarm clock indicated Mass had just finished. Maybe Dad thought the good Lord would substitute our attendance of Mom's funeral Mass for attending today.

Touching his paw to my nose, I pulled Spooky into my arms and petted him hoping for a few more minutes in bed. I thought of Mom. I missed the aroma of fresh coffee, fried bacon, and eggs she prepared on weekends.

Her illness had been lengthy, slowly draining her life. As her condition had worsened and she'd been admitted to the hospital, I'd tried to prepare myself for her death. I'd known it was coming, but when reality had presented itself, I still wasn't ready. I missed the times she would chime in with a comment, offer her advice, but most of all I missed her laugh, her voice. Her death made me realize that one is never quite prepared for the finality of losing a loved one.

I rose, set Spooky on the floor, and headed toward the bathroom with my clothes for the day cradled in my arm. I stepped into the hot water of the shower and was thankful my boss had given me the week off with pay. My reward for being a reliable employee? More than likely he was allowing me time to grieve, pull myself together.

With my senior year of high school starting soon, I wondered if Dad wanted my help sorting through Mom's things and bagging them up for donations to charities. Maybe we would do that today, but then again it may be too soon for him to do so, and for me as well. Dressed, I went downstairs. He was sitting at the kitchen table staring into his cup of coffee, looking a bit dazed, or perhaps daydreaming of happier times. *Did he make coffee?*

"Good morning." I took a mug from the cupboard and helped myself to a cup of coffee.

As if my greeting had interrupted his thoughts, he looked surprised to see me.

"Morning." He took a sip from his coffee cup. "How are you this morning?"

I shrugged my shoulders. I didn't know how I felt. Sad, depressed, empty, apprehensive, or maybe even scared. I avoided answering his question and posed one of my own.

"When did you want to sort through Mom's things? You know, donate them to charity."

Dad didn't answer. He stared down into his coffee mug again. It was all the answer I needed. He wasn't ready to let go of her belongings. I'd hoped we could put the task behind us, doing it quickly like pulling off a band-aid.

He drained the last of his coffee, rose, and kissed the top of my head.

"Not today. There's no rush. We have plenty of time to do it later." He placed his coffee cup in the dishwasher and left the room.

FROM BEYOND THE GRAVE

My brother, still in bed, was taking full advantage of us missing church today. Being the CEO of his lawn service business, a summer job and title he'd created, it was his policy not to work on weekends when customers had gatherings and cookouts. He understood the disruption of a noisy lawnmower during such activities was unwelcomed. Pretty mature policy for a soon to be sophomore in high school. He'd mentioned leaving the responsibility of his business in the hands of his partners for a few days. He needed time to grieve as well.

I made myself some toast and ate a banana. *A whole week.* I sipped on my coffee. *What am I going to do?* I needed a project to occupy my mind and distract it from the emptiness within my heart.

Spooky stood at the back door, turned toward me, and meowed.

I looked at the demanding feline.

"OK, I'm coming." Taking my coffee cup with me, I opened the door and stepped into the sunshine as the cat scampered onto the deck. Tilting my face skyward to the warmness of the sun, I wondered if Mom's soul was in Heaven and if she could see me. I scanned the yard. The leafy trees swayed in the gentle breeze. My eyes paused at the disheveled flower garden. As if drawn to it by an invisible force, I went to the gate, opened it, and stood before the flowers crowded by weeds.

15

"Well, Mom, challenge accepted. Maybe you can guide my hands to distinguish the difference between a weed and a flower."

I went into the garage, set my empty coffee cup by the back door, put on a pair of her gardening gloves that were laying on a shelf, and selected a spade. I found a bushel basket lying on the cement floor, the one Mom had used for the weeds she pulled.

Entering through the arbor, I sighed. The pathways were cluttered with greenery. Whatever they were, weed or flower, they needed to go. I squatted and began digging and pulling. My plan was to work to clear the pathways, before moving on to the interior beds. Upset by my intrusion, the birds who had taken up residence in the four birdhouses were busy bringing bugs or whatever else they could find to feed their young.

"Planning to weed it?" Came a voice from above.

I looked over the picket fence to see our neighbor's smiling, wrinkled face shaded by her large-rimed straw hat. She had a pair of gloves and a spade in her hands.

"I hope so. I'm not very good at knowing what to pull but thought it would be safe to begin in the pathways."

"Would you like some help?"

"I could use your advice. I'm certain you know better than I what needs to be done."

My neighbor was patient and shared her vast knowledge as we spent most of the morning identifying plants and weeds.

Even though I avoided the subject, she was compelled to talk about Mom.

"You know, your mother really loved this garden."

"Yes. She referred to her flowers as nature's canvas and she was the painter."

"She had a talent for it indeed." Her elderly hands pulled another weed and tossed it into the basket.

"Mom mentioned you helping her pull weeds from time to time. I know she appreciated your help especially when her health began to fail."

"It's the neighborly thing to do. Your mother would have done the same for me." She tossed another weed aside. "I don't like to be sick either. It's so limiting and frustrating. Toward the end of her life, I felt it was more important to spend time with her then to tend her garden. I know it was difficult for her to be unable to work out here and watch from her window as the weeds overtook its beauty. Between you and I, we should be able to restore the garden to the way she had it before."

"Hello, ladies." Dad carried a tray of food through the arbor.

I pushed my glove away from my watch. It was after 12:30. Goodness! We had worked for over three hours.

"Thanks, Dad." I stood. I dropped my spade to the ground, took off the garden gloves, and let them fall on top of the spade.

Dad set the tray on the white iron table in the center of the garden, turned, and held up two damp washcloths.

"I thought you would want to wash your hands before you eat."

"Good thinking." I looked at the bits of dead brown plants and seeds that had found their way inside my gloves and stuck to my sweaty hands.

Our neighbor set her gardening gloves and spade on the ground near the weed basket.

"That's thoughtful of you. Thank you." She accepted the damp washcloth. "I hope you will be joining us."

"If you don't mind." Dad looked at the tray. "I've brought enough for all of us."

Our neighbor motioned toward an empty chair.

"Please." She smiled as she inspected the food on the tray. "It looks delicious." She pulled out a chair and sat.

Dad sat in a chair opposite our neighbor. As I sat, he handed me a washcloth. I scanned the tray of food he had brought as I wiped my hands. A pitcher of lemonade, sandwiches, I assumed ham and cheese, a bag of chips, grapes, and a few store-bought cookies. I stopped wiping my hands as a pang pierced my heart. My mother's homemade cookies. I'd forgotten to bake and replenish our never-ending stock of chocolate chip cookies Mom kept in the freezer.

Dad poured a glass of lemonade and set it before me.

"Honey, are you OK?" Dad held out his hand to accept our used washcloths and set them on the seat of the empty chair.

I faked a smile but was certain he recognized my weak attempt.

"Yes." I watched as a bead of condensation dripped down the side of my glass. Was it really that hot outside? I looked at my neighbor. Her face was flushed. I hoped she hadn't overdone it.

I picked up my glass and drank half of it.

"Oh, that's good, Dad."

He smiled as he bit into his sandwich.

We kept our conversation light with shared memories of Mom, her thoughtful planning of the garden plants, and the needed upkeep. I recalled the day she had discovered a snake amongst the pile of rocks she had set aside to outline each flowerbed. She had reached for a stone, only to discover a brown, beige, and red colored snake warming itself among them. She hadn't been certain if it was poisonous, so she'd kept me and my brother far away from it. Our cat at the time, Thomas, had to be put in the house. The snake wasn't happy about us discovering his new home, so it slithered away.

Dad drank the last of his lemonade and placed his empty dishes upon the tray.

"It's getting pretty hot out here. Maybe you two should call it a day, or at least wait until after dinner once the sun gets lower in the sky."

I looked at my neighbor. She was older than Mom, maybe in her 70s, and I knew she wouldn't quit until I did.

"I think that may be a good idea. It's quite warm and humid today."

Our neighbor nodded her head in agreement. She glanced at the empty clothesline in her back yard.

"I have laundry to do, and with it being such a nice day, it should dry quickly." She drank the last of her lemonade and placed her glass and plate on the tray. I did the same.

She was the only person in the neighborhood with a clothesline in her backyard. Kind of old fashioned, but maybe she was just set in her ways, preferred her clothes with a fresh air fragrance, or it helped lower her gas bill. She retrieved her gloves and spade from the weed basket as I retrieved mine and picked up the basket by the wire handle.

She turned to Dad.

"Thank you for the delicious lunch. It was nice to eat with someone for a change."

"You're welcome." Dad picked up the tray.

I looked toward her as she walked through the arbor and headed across our yard with Dad following with the tray.

"Thank you for your help. I've learned a lot from you today." I paused at the garage as she continued toward her house and waved her hand over her shoulder.

"Any time, any time."

After leaving the basket of weeds outside the garage and putting away the gloves and spade, Spooky scooted past me as I retrieved my coffee cup and followed Dad into the house. Established as our household protocol, he kicked off his shoes in the mudroom. I did the same before joining him at the kitchen sink. He handed me a rinsed dish, which I placed inside the dishwasher.

"Thanks for lunch, Dad."

"My pleasure." He took a scrap of ham from a plate and dropped it on the floor for Spooky. "It was nice of her to come over and help you. Such a nice lady."

I watched as the cat ate the meat. He seemed hungry even though we always had dry food in a dish for him. Had he lost weight too? Was he beginning to show his age?

"Yes, we've always been able to rely on her for help when we needed it." I accepted another rinsed plate and filed it with the others. "I remember her telling Mom that her husband died of a heart attack within six months after his retirement. I always thought it was so sad. He worked all of his life and just when he could begin enjoying it, he died."

"It seems unfair, but maybe it was his time to go."

"She must be lonely. Even though she attends church regularly, I don't think she is involved in any related activities."

Dad put the leftover grapes and pitcher of lemonade into the refrigerator while I put the three glasses and my coffee cup into the dishwasher.

I sighed. "I'm glad Mom took the time to visit with her."

"Me too. Who would have known that your mother's time was so limited and valuable?"

A New Normalcy

A sparrow landed on the windowsill, drawing my attention. I looked to the bird feeders. They were empty. Dang squirrel was eating more than his fair share again. The greedy little guy would help himself to a chunk of suet, hang upside down by his toes, and proudly flash his bulbous belly while he ate. Mom always chucked at the silly sight.

I wasn't sure if my brother had come out of hibernation yet today. Even though he knew how to do his own laundry, a task Mom had insisted we learn, I washed, dried, and folded the communal pile in the laundry room.

With the clean clothes stacked in the basket, I carried it upstairs and sorted them into piles on my bed.

I went to Dad's bedroom and stood for a moment with his stack of clothes in my arms. Mom's perfume lingered in the air. I inhaled its fragrance before placing his clothes on his bed. I looked to her side of the bed, vacant, where she had spent several of her last months before going to the hospital.

Scooping up my brother's clothes from my bed, I went to his bedroom and stood before his closed door. I could hear him talking to the TV. More than likely he was playing a video game. I knocked.

"Come in." His voice was monotone.

As I had assumed, his long legs hung over the side of his bed, the controller in his hand. He had undergone a growth spurt lately. Even though he was my little brother, I was now looking up to him.

"Here are your clothes." I set them on the end of his bed. He moved his head to one side in order to continue to see the TV.

"Thanks, Sis."

"When are you going back to work?"

"Tomorrow."

So soon. I thought he was taking a few days off. I looked around his unkept room; bed wasn't made, clothes on the floor.

"You planning to stay in here all day?"

He put the game on pause and gave me a sly look, half smiling.

"No, I need to get something to eat soon."

"Speaking of eating, any idea what you want to eat for dinner?" I don't know why I asked. His reply was always the same.

"Pizza." He pressed the button on his controller and continued with his video game.

I closed his door as I left and returned to my room. It was quiet, too quiet, which allowed my mind to drift to Mom and her funeral. I looked at the framed photograph of her and me on my nightstand and sighed. No longer able to withstand the crushing silence, I turned on the TV and busied myself with putting my clothes away.

With my brother returning to work tomorrow, I thought it would be best to return to work as well. I would call my boss in the morning and ask to be put back on the schedule. With school starting soon, I wanted to put in as many hours as possible before trying to juggle work, classes, and sports.

However, I wasn't looking forward to facing my boss and coworkers. The last thing I wanted was for people to tell me they were sorry for my loss. In truth, I was afraid I would burst into tears, embarrassing myself. I guessed they would understand if I did, but I hoped I could remain strong, emotionless. I was tired of crying, tired of being sad. I wanted my life to get back to normal, but I knew in my heart it would never be the same.

I busied myself making a double batch of Mom's chocolate chip cookies. They weren't as good as her cookies, but then again, food always tasted better when someone else

25

made it. There were enough cookies to fill two plastic containers. Knowing Dad and my brother would eat a batch before they could go stale, I kept one container on the counter and the other went into the freezer. Nothing like a frozen chocolate chip cookie on a hot summer day. You can bite off a piece of the cookie, and let it defrost in your mouth until the chocolate chips melt.

I went back to the flower garden and continued to clear the pathway until it was time to call in the order for dinner. I showered to remove the dirt and sweat from the day before the pizza arrived.

As the aroma of freshly baked pizza drifted up to his bedroom, my brother emerged and joined Dad and me at the kitchen table. He piled half of the large pizza onto his plate.

I'm glad I ordered two large pizzas and a salad. I watched in disbelief as he picked up the first piece, folded it in half and bit off the pointed end halfway to the crust.

"I guess you're hungry."

He didn't bother to answer, only nodded.

With dinner out of the way, fatigue crept into my body. Maybe it was from working in the heat while weeding the garden. I paused before the window to admire my progress. Most of the pathways were clear. *I promise, Mom, I'll get it restored to its full beauty.* As the sun dipped below the horizon, I changed into my pajamas, brushed my teeth, and got into bed.

FROM BEYOND THE GRAVE

I picked up the book from my nightstand. I had borrowed from Mom's library last week. A historical romance, my favorite.

After reading for several hours, my eyelids began to close. Setting the book on my nightstand, I ensured my cell phone was plugged in to charge. I picked it up, flipped through the pictures until I came upon a video of Mom and me. I pressed play. It was good to hear her voice again. I smiled through my tears and was thankful for the captured memory. Returning my phone to the nightstand, I snuggled under the blankets.

I smiled as I wiped a tear from my cheek. We'd shared such good times; shopping for clothes, antiques, and treating ourselves to lunch. We often phoned each other throughout the day, that is, until she'd lost her hearing, then we would text. When she became weak, even that stopped. I wondered. Was she happy, safe, no longer in pain, alone or with others, and more than anything, I wondered if she could see me? Was she near me, in another dimension? Did she have a magic mirror to peer into and see me whenever she wanted? Did she eat food? I knew that sounded silly, but when you are dead, yet your soul is alive, do you eat? I guessed I would find out one day.

With thoughts whirling around in my head, I drifted off to sleep.

*   *   *

I woke the next morning. After showering, dressing, and eating breakfast, I called my boss.

"I need you to put me back on the schedule."

"Are you sure? You know you're being paid while you are off."

"I know, but I just need to stay busy. I really want to put in as many hours as I can before school begins too."

She paused, almost hesitant to reply.

"I see. Well, let me check the schedule. Hang on." She put me on hold knowing she needed to ask those working if they would be willing to give up a shift.

"Does a shift on Wednesday and Thursday work for you?"

"Yes, that would be great."

"Good. I'll pencil you in."

"Thanks, and can I ask a favor?"

"Sure."

"I don't want anyone to make a big deal out of my mother's death. It will be difficult for me to come back as it is, but everyone saying they are sorry and too many hugs of sympathy may put me over my emotional threshold. I don't want to embarrass myself."

"I can't stop them from doing what makes them feel better in dealing with the situation, but I'll mention it to them."

"Thanks. I'll see you in a few days." I sighed. The house was quiet. Dad and my brother were at work. I was alone, well, except for the cat. I assumed he had been fed even though he begged for a portion of my scrambled eggs as I sat stood by the counter and ate them.

Entering the living room with my coffee in hand, I ran my finger over Mom's desk leaving a line in the dust. I couldn't remember the last time the house had had a thorough cleaning. *And just when I thought I wouldn't have anything to do today.*

I cleaned the house, made dinner, and set the table including folded napkins and the salt and pepper shakers. We always seemed to forget the salt and pepper. Moments later, Dad and my brother arrived home.

Dad scanned the readied meal as he sat down to eat.

"Wow, this looks great!"

My brother emerged from the bathroom after washing his hands. He had grass clippings on his shirt and pants. *So much for cleaning the house.*

"This looks good, sis. I'm starving."

When wasn't he starving? My dinner was nothing special, just spaghetti with meat sauce, garlic bread, green beans, and cookies for dessert. I was glad I made a large amount of spaghetti. My brother filled his plate several times and ate close to a dozen cookies with two glasses of milk before sitting back in his chair with a satisfied sigh.

After each of us rinsed our plates and silverware and placed them in the dishwasher, I washed the pots and pans, Dad dried and put them away before going to pay the bills. It seemed as if the hospital had wasted little time in wanting their share of his money.

Our lives seemed a little normal, a little mundane, and a little empty.

I looked around the tidy kitchen before going to my room. I wanted to go through my clothes for school and weed out some to donate to the church outreach program.

I turned on the lamp, grabbed the remote from my nightstand, and clicked on the TV. After surfing through several channels to discover nothing of interest to watch, I settled on a show about the history of something.

I opened the top drawer of my dresser, sorted through my underwear, and tossed several pairs of panties into my wastebasket. I jotted down the number to be replaced on a shopping list. *On to socks.* I dumped the drawer onto my bed and inspected each pair for a hole in the big toe. I always seemed to get a hole in the big toes. *Maybe I should cut my toenails more often.* Next, folded shirts. After trying to sort through them, I kept them all. Pajamas, I threw out a few ratty ones. I opened my closet. I had a few items I had hung onto since middle school; they went into the donation bag. I tried on my jeans and dress slacks. They still fit. *Yeah, no weight gain.* Ah, the dresses. I discovered I couldn't get rid of any of them as they brought back memories of Mom and I shopping together. The welling tears cascaded down my cheeks. *Perhaps another time.* I closed the closet doors.

I changed into my pajamas, brushed my teeth, and got into bed. I paused before shutting off my lamp to look at the picture of Mom and me. I picked it up and touched my mother's face. Tears welled again.

"Good night, Mom. I love and miss you."

Grief is strange. One minute you're fine, the next you can't stop crying. It overtakes you in waves as if you are blindfolded lying on the beach with the water repeatedly and unexpectantly crashing into you. At first, the frequency is often, but over time, I prayed the waves would have a greater interval between them, until they subsided into calmness.

Maybe a run in the morning would do me some good.

I wiped the tears from my cheeks and returned the picture to my nightstand. I set my alarm, clicked off the TV, and turned out the light with the hope of drifting off to sleep and dreaming of happier times.

Reiteration

I watched a younger man, who stood before the gentle-faced spirit. He reminded me of my son, maybe younger. The teenager listened carefully to what He told him. With confusion masking his face, he looked to his spirit guide for clarification and nodded before he gave his reply to Him. In an instant, the teenager and his spirit guide vanished.

I turned to my spirit guide.

"Where did they go?"

"The young man may have made a choice to return to his physical life. Or he may have been brought here to relay a message to a loved one, or even a stranger."

"I see. An afterlife experience, so to speak?"

"*Yes. More than likely the young man still had a purpose to fulfill.*"

I looked to where the teenager and his spirit guide once stood.

"Am I allowed to return to my family?"

"*Your purpose has been fulfilled. You may return, but only in spirit form. They will not be able to see you.*"

"What time is it there?"

"*In their time, it has been three days since your death. Time is much slower here. If you wish to visit them, they are sleeping now. Imagine it and it shall be.*"

A message from Him pictured within my mind. The future? Her future? My husband's future? Panic like a bolt of lightning resonated within my soul. I looked at my spirit guide, who nodded his head.

"*He feels it is necessary to instill the dream a second time.*"

"A second time?"

"Yes."

I closed my eyes and thought of Elizabeth. Opening my eyes, I stood in her bedroom. She was lying in bed, sleeping peacefully. I looked at the corner of her bedroom where her spirit guide hovered. I smiled and nodded my head slightly before turning to my spirit guide.

"Am I able to see everyone's spirit guide now?"

"Yes."

As before, I stepped beside Elizabeth's bed to convey the dream once again.

~

Dad lay on the couch in the family room. I sat in the large leather chair with my feet on the ataman. We were watching TV. I looked toward him and saw a rectangular mirror on the wall near his head. It didn't have a frame. In fact, I wasn't certain how it was attached to the wall. I found it strange that he was unaware of it being there.

I stared as I saw a hand pass through the mirror and extend toward Dad. It handed him something that looked like a small stack of playing cards, but they had notches on each corner like a larger version of the tickets used for a 50/50 drawing at local sporting events. Dad accepted them absentmindedly, as if it was almost a reflex. I watched as he fanned them out in his hands like he was playing cards. They were tickets.

The top ticket was black framed along the edge with a thin line of white. The second card was red trimmed as the previous ticket. There were other tickets too, four in all, but I didn't see them. I somehow knew they existed and were various colors; yellow and blue.

I watched the empty hand withdraw and disappear into the mirror and saw Mom staring back at me. Her hair was

34

perfectly styled, her favorite shade of lipstick on her lips, and she had on a white angora scoop neck sweater. She looked directly at me, smiling.

"Mom!" She looked so pretty, a little younger too.

"*I'm happy and I am OK.*" She spoke without moving her lips, yet I heard the message within my mind. I understood. She had crossed over and was fine.

She scrunched her shoulders upward, raised her right hand, and wiggled her fingers toward me as she waved good-bye.

~

I shut off my alarm and lay in bed recalling every facet of the dream. *It was Mom, I know it was her.* A peaceful feeling came over me. *Her wave, it was even her wave.* I recalled the countless photos capturing her signature wave. But the dream, this haunting dream, seemed familiar. I had dreamed it before. *Tickets? Maybe Dad will know what they are.*

I donned my running attire, headed for the kitchen, and grabbed a banana from the fruit basket.

Dad walked into the kitchen, grabbed his travel mug, and filled it with coffee. He looked like he was running late.

I pulled back the banana peel.

"Good morning." I bit into the fruit.

Dad glanced up quickly as he set the coffee pot back on the stand.

"Morning, sweetie. You're going for a run."

"Yes. Though it may do me some good to get a little exercise this morning."

"I wish I could join you, but I'm already running late for work, no pun intended." He pushed the top on his travel mug in place before cutting a slice from the coffee cake and placing it on a paper towel.

Even though he may not take my dream seriously, I wanted his opinion.

"Dad, I had a dream about Mom. In fact, this is the second time I have had it. It's a bit strange and I wonder if you know what it means."

He grabbed the handle of his laptop bag, balanced the coffee cake on the top of his travel mug, and kissed the top of my head as he went to the door.

"Can we talk about it when I get home tonight?"

"Sure." The slam of the storm door echoed within the kitchen as I threw my banana peel in the trash. I retrieved my phone and house keys from my room, fed Spooky his portion of canned cat food, and put on my tennis shoes. My brother's work boots were missing. I assumed he'd started his day early in order to work in the cooler morning temperatures. I locked the kitchen door and stepped onto the sidewalk.

FROM BEYOND THE GRAVE

I turned my face toward the sunny sky, dotted with clouds, as I stretched to warm up. I remembered when I was little, Mom and I would lay in the grass and look at the clouds. We would imagine them as shapes, sometimes animals. Was she among the clouds now?

Bending to touch my toes, a white feather rolled on the ground near my shoe, yet I did not feel a breeze. Grasping it, I rolled the feather between my thumb and forefinger and looked to the trees. They were still.

I once read an article about a woman who used to see dragonflies wherever she went; on walks, while shopping, and even outside her office window. She believed they were a sign from her mother as if she'd stopped by for a visit. My friend who lost her grandmother said she always found coins on the floor, and was often visited by a bluebird.

Recalling the white feather on my mother's desk, I decided right then and there that my mother was doing the same. Whenever she was near, she would let me know by leaving a feather.

"Thank you, Mom." I tucked the feather into my pocket, jogged down the driveway, and onto the sidewalk.

We lived on the outskirts of town, a mile away from the park. The historic streets were lined with large maple trees and the architecture of the houses reflected the time period when the community had been founded. Many of the houses dated back to when Lincoln was president, some were even older.

I rounded the corner onto the main street. My normal trek downhill into town was a nice easy jog with a challenging return trip toward home. Countless times, even at a young age, Mom and I had walked to town. I looked at the candy store as I passed it and remembered her purchasing surprise bags for me and my brother. Out of breath and apparently out of shape, I stopped in the park to rest on a bench. As the sound of water resonates over the dam, I looked to the rushing water remembering the time my fishing pole had broken because I had hooked a large carp. I looked to the swings that Mom used to push me on them when I was little. My eyes welled with tears.

*   *   *

"She looks sad." I stood in the park across from Elizabeth. "I hoped the feather would let her know I was near."

"*She misses you.*"

"Unfortunately, there isn't much I can do about it."

"*You may use that woman's body and give her another sign of your presence.*"

I looked to the woman, about the same age as me when I died, approaching a bench across from Elizabeth.

"How?"

"*You may use her body to project your face, but only long enough for her to believe she has seen you.*"

"She has to look at me though, right?"

"*Yes, and she will. You will have control of the woman's movement.*"

I went to the bench and sat just before the woman sat on top of me pressing my spirit into her body. I turned my head, the woman's head, and looked to my daughter.

*   *   *

I watched as a woman sat upon a bench and turned her head to look at me. *Mom?* I blinked my eyes clearing away my tears, but the woman's face seemed to change. It wasn't Mom after all, but for a split second, I could swear it was her or at least resembled her.

I tried to distract my mind by thinking of something else, but it could not be swayed. The threatening tears brimmed over the edge of my eyes. I wiped them away and got up from the bench.

*   *   *

I stood from the woman's body and she brushed her arms as if trying to dust them off. I moved next to my spirit guide and watched Elizabeth leave the park.

"My presence seems to have made her sadder."

"*She will be fine in time.*"

"I believe she recognized me though. I could see it in her eyes." Even though my appearance had been for only a second or two, I hoped she had understood that I was near, that I was fine. I watched as she disappeared around the corner of a building and continued homeward.

"*Yes. The living may be incapable of recognizing our ability to use their bodies for our purpose. If necessary, we can pass through them as well. When this occurs, they feel as if they have encountered a spiderweb and quickly brush it away from their body. Other times, they may feel as if their head has bumped into something, duck, and look up, only to find nothing there. They usually smooth their hair thinking it needs to be put back in place. They may even experience a cold spot or a breeze pass by them and look to see if a door or window is open.*"

I looked around the park. The last time I was here, my spirit guide had transformed into a protective guardian when he sensed danger. It made me wonder.

"Will you always be with me?"

"*Yes.*"

"Even during my next life?"

"*I have been with you from your very first life and will continue to do so until you have learned all you need to learn. At that time, you will decide what you shall do.*"

I looked toward him.

"Thank you. Even though I cannot see you while living a physical life, I appreciate your guidance and protection."

He bowed his head in acknowledgment.

*   *   *

I found a large vase in the kitchen cupboard and decided to keep it in my bedroom, high on a shelf of my bookcase, away from Spooky's reach. I dropped the two feathers inside it. After a quick shower and a change of clothes, I passed my parents' bedroom door on the way downstairs, but paused for a moment. I stepped inside their room, opened the closet door, and inhaled the fragrance of Mom's perfume. It was more than I could bear. I slid down the doorframe until I sat upon the carpet with tears rolling down my face. Wrapping my arms around my stomach as if hugging myself, I sat and let the ache in my heart release its burden of grief. I was glad to be alone with no one to witness my meltdown.

When I was able to pull myself together, I got up from the floor and began to go through her clothes. I found the softest sweater on a shelf and held it to my nose. Her fragrance made her seem near. I took the sweater, went to my room, and placed it under my pillow.

"Oh, I really need to get back to work and get my mind on something else."

Conveying The Message

I had dinner ready when Dad arrived home. It was just the two of us. Apparently, my brother was working late.

"Ah, my favorite." He pulled out a chair and sat down. I joined him.

Our meal consisted of meatloaf, mashed potatoes with gravy, corn muffins, and carrots. I was quite confident the carrots, potatoes, and gravy would taste fine especially since the carrots and gravy came from a can. The muffins came from a mix. I had just followed the directions on the box. However, the meatloaf was questionable. It didn't quite look like when Mom had made it, and I wasn't certain what spices I should add, but after a quick internet search, I'd chosen the recipe I thought would taste best.

Dad scanned the table.

"Salt and pepper?"

Dang, forgot it.

"I'll get it." I rose to retrieve them. "Dad, I've been having dreams since Mom died." I reached into the cupboard and retrieved the two shakers.

"You have?" He lifted a slice of meatloaf from the pan and put it on his plate.

"Yes." I placed the shakers on the table next to his plate. He picked up the salt before looking at me curiously indicating I should continue.

"I had a dream before Mom's funeral. She told me not to be afraid." I waited for his reaction. He glanced at me before taking a bite of meatloaf. "I think she tried to warn me about the strange beam of light. Remember me nudging you when I saw it?"

He paused with a forkful of carrots in midair and a puzzled expression upon his face. "I didn't see any light." He shoveled the carrots into his mouth.

"You didn't see it?"

He shook his head while he chewed.

Strange. Was I the only one who had seen the beam of light?

"Well, I did. It was coming through the ceiling, but it was only there for a short time before it disappeared."

"Maybe it was a reflection of some kind, like from a buckle or watch."

He had a point, but I was certain it was more than that.

"Anyway, I had a dream about her again last night. You were in the dream too."

He glanced at me as he cut a bite of meatloaf with the edge of his fork. "Oh really? What was the dream about?"

"You and I were watching TV in the family room. I was sat in the chair and you were lying on the couch. A mirror that didn't have a frame was on the wall close to your head. A hand came from the mirror and handed you four tickets. They were big, like playing cards, but they were notched at the corners like the ones on a roll of 50/50 raffle tickets." I paused to make sure he was listening as he continued to eat.

"Ya, go on."

"You fanned them out in your hand like when we play poker. The top one was black. It was white around the edge. The second ticket was red trimmed in white, and I knew there were other tickets of different colors, but I didn't see them. I think there were four in all. I watched as the hand went back into the mirror and saw Mom staring at me."

Dad stopped chewing. I had his undivided attention and continued.

"She looked healthy. Her hair was perfect, and she even had on her favorite shade of lipstick. I only saw her from her shoulders on up, like a school picture, but she had on a scooped neck, white angora sweater. She smiled at me as if she knew I could see her. She didn't move her lips, but I understood that she was happy and fine. Before my alarm rang, she scrunched her shoulders and waved just like she always did, wiggling her fingers. We have so many pictures of her in that pose. It's like her signature wave. It had to be her."

Dad began to chew again. He swallowed before he spoke.

"Well, at least we know she's happy and fine."

He acted as if the dream meant nothing at all, dismissing it easily. Did he think I was making this up? Did he think I was reading too much into it?

"Then you believe me?"

"I do believe you, but it's just a dream. We all have dreams. Maybe it was just your subconscious. We've had a lot to deal with over the past couple of months with her illness and passing."

"But what do the four tickets mean?"

"Were they lottery tickets?"

"No, they were tickets."

"To what?"

"I don't know. I just know they were tickets, four tickets."

He took another helping of meatloaf and placed it on his plate.

"As I said, it's just a dream."

So, concluded our conversation on the topic. I sighed, a bit dejected knowing there was more to it than he was willing to believe.

My Senior Year

It seemed strange to have Dad take our traditional first day of school picture. With him usually at work, Mom had taken it in the past. After he took the photo, I looked down to my shoe to see a tiny white feather. I smiled. *Thank you, Mom.* I ran up the stairs and deposited the feather in my vase. My brother had obtained his driver's license and purchased a good used car during the summer, so we drove separately to school.

My friends were sympathetic to my loss as we gathered before class. I thanked them kindly, tried to keep a smile on my face, and focused on my schedule loaded with advanced placement classes. I was determined to pass all of them in order to receive as many college credits as possible.

Days became a blur as September went by quickly. When I wasn't studying, I was working or trying to keep the house in order. I attended as many home football games as my work schedule allowed and was able to go to the homecoming dance with friends.

October was my favorite month, with its colors of autumn, and kicking the rustling leaves during my run or walk in town, and Halloween, but it was a particularly difficult month for all of us. Not only was October Mom's favorite month, but midmonth was also her birthday. In remembrance, I made a birthday cake and we sang 'Happy Birthday' to Mom hoping she was celebrating wherever she was. I was glad I was able to get through the song without crying, but later in my room I allowed the tears I'd held back to fall.

I was relieved when Grandma offered to have us to her house for Thanksgiving. The thought of making a turkey and large dinner by myself was intimidating. I went to her house early in the morning to help make dinner and learn a few pointers for future reference.

Decorating the house for Christmas fell upon my shoulders. Dad made his usual contribution. He set up our tree and put the angel on top. I chose not to hang Mom's stocking on the fireplace. After all, there wouldn't be anything in it on Christmas morning. I found Mom's recipes, made a variety of cookies, and did my best to hid them in the freezer so I only had to make each batch once. I remembered the year Dad had eaten an entire batch of his favorite cookie a week before Christmas. Mom had been so mad. She'd had to make a second batch and had warned Dad not to eat any of them until she served them on the platter Christmas morning.

With our gifts wrapped and under the tree, the three of us attended Midnight Mass, my favorite Mass of the year. I loved the church, decorated in all its splendor, and the choir leading us in Christmas Carols, the fragrance of incense drifting in a haze from the altar, and our community gathered together. I had cheese and crackers prepared as a snack when we returned home from the service. While we ate, we watched a Christmas movie before going to bed.

Christmas morning, we opened our gifts before going to Grandma's house for dinner. Except for Mom's empty chair where she sat throughout the day, it was a typical Christmas. A little melancholy, but typical.

I'd thought I would have found a feather or even had a dream during the past few months, but I had not. Was Mom no longer near me?

I worked additional hours and studied for my midterm exams during the remainder of Christmas break. The day after the new year, I packed the decorations into their boxes and put them away. In a way, it was a relief to put behind us the difficult, first holidays without Mom.

My senior year of high school was going by quickly. Midterm exams were complete, and my last semester of high school commenced. Fighting off senioritis, I was ready to move on with my life leaving school, teachers, and many of my classmates behind. I looked forward to going away to study, to be on my own, and responsible for just me. To think I could do my laundry when I wanted, eat when I wanted, and select the classes I wanted for each semester. I wasn't certain of my major, but I knew I had until the end of my sophomore year to declare it.

For now, I was looking forward to the three of us leaving for spring break on Saturday. My suitcase was laying open on my bedroom floor, and I just needed to throw in a few last-minute items. The examined the list laying on my dresser with its remaining entries yet to be crossed off. *One more day of school.* I got into bed. *I just need to get through tomorrow.* I shut off my lamp and went to sleep.

*   *   *

I paced at the end of Elizabeth's bed.

"Why does she need to know what is to come? She will not be involved."

"*It isn't necessary, but it will strengthen the communication between you. She will perceive this message and entrust future messages from you.*"

"How do we know this future event will happen?"

"*It is preordained, just as one's life is preordained. But unlike this unfortunate event, one may change their pathway in life with choices they make. This cannot be avoided.*"

"But what about those who are attending? They may get injured or even die. Have they made a choice to do so?"

"*In a way, they have decided by attending the event, thus accepting the consequences of their choice.*"

I stood next to Elizabeth's bed, looked at her peaceful face, and concentrated while conveying my thoughts and images.

~

I was standing on the center dashed line of a blacktop street in a large city, larger than my home town, but where was I? There were tall buildings on each side of the road. People lined the streets, lots of people. They were cheering for others who were on the street. Several passed by me. Did I see a park to my right? Trees anyways. It was difficult to tell. Suddenly, an explosion shook the ground. I covered my ears as a second explosion sounded to my right. The acrid smoke lingered in the air. I heard screaming, and people were dazed, picking themselves up off the blacktop and sidewalks. Through the fogginess, I saw others laying on the ground. Carnage, chaos, and panic surrounded me as people scattered in fright, while others rushed toward the injured and dying. Paramedics with wheelchairs, stretchers, and cases of medical supplies ran forward. Several people volunteered to help the injured. I stood and watched as people gathered around the victims to assist where they could.

~

I shut off my alarm, wiped the sleep from my eyes, and sat up. *What a horrible dream.* It played over again in my mind while I readied for school.

I met my friend, one of only two that I had, at my locker. "I have to tell you about this dream I had. It seemed so real." Shutting my locker, we walked to class.

She raised her eyebrows as if curious as to what I would say. "Ok..."

"I was standing in the center of a blacktop road, right on the dashed line, and I was in a city. I knew this because there were tall buildings on each side of the street. There were people lining the street like for an event or parade, but then there were these two explosions to my right. It was terrible. There was panic, chaos. People were hurt, maybe even dead. Then my alarm went off."

She looked toward me as we entered our first hour classroom.

"Sounds more like a nightmare to me."

I had a seat in the front of the class, she was three seats behind me. I pushed the dream from my mind and tried to focus on the teacher's instructions for the test.

As the day progressed, I counted down each hour, each minute, before being released for spring break. I imagined the warm rays of sunshine bronzing my body as I lay on the white sand of the beach. I was fortunate to be going to a warmer climate. I knew other families could not afford to do so.

Spring Break

Ah, Saturday. Let spring break begin!

The three of us caught an early flight to Florida. My brother wanted the aisle seat, I preferred the window, and Dad was kind enough to let us have our wish and sat between us. I knew it seemed a little strange for me, a Senior in high school, to spend spring break with my family, but I didn't care much for the drinking or the peer pressure that went along with the party scene. I cringed inside when hearing the tales from upper classmen's wild and crazy spring break experiences; drinking themselves into a stupor, sleeping around, being so drunk that they stripped and danced on tabletops, and smoking pot.

54

FROM BEYOND THE GRAVE

Our plane landed, we rented a car, and were off to locate the house we'd rented for the week.

I set my duffle bag in the foyer of the three-bedroom ranch.

"Wow, this is nice." I toured the house. It had a screened in pool. *Yeah, no bugs.* A lizard thing scurried along the outside of the screen. *They're cute, but I don't want them crawling on me while I'm sunbathing.*

We each claimed a bedroom before our trip to the grocery store. We agreed to have a large breakfast every morning, eat snacks at the beach or around the pool, and then cook on the grill or go out for dinner in the evening. I had taken the time to plan the meals we would cook during our stay, made a list of necessary ingredients, and divided them equally on three shopping lists, thus turning our mundane task into our annual scavenger hunt. Since we were unfamiliar with the grocery store, we each took a cart and raced to find the items on our list. The first one back to the checkout was the winner. Dad usually took his time and always found additional items that weren't on his list, so the race was usually between me and my brother.

Once the groceries were purchased and put away, we changed into our bathing suits, grabbed the sunscreen, towels, munchies, and went straight to the pool.

Ah. I sighed as my body relaxed in the warmth of the sun. I'd discovered a natural sunscreen a few years ago and, much to my surprise, it really worked. I opened the cap and began to cover my body with a protective coating. After Mom's death, I'd changed my lifestyle. No GMO products, less sugar, exercise, and I'd reduced as many chemicals in my life as possible.

We ate dinner out that night. We were too tired and lazy from traveling and relaxing in the sun to cook.

After breakfast the next morning, we packed a cooler and went to the beach. Oh, I really love to walk along the shore, pick up sea shells, and look at the oceanfront hotels.

Dinner was chicken on the grill and fresh corn accompanied by an evening of watching TV or scanning social media websites via our cellphones. I received a few text messages from my friend, which included videos of the wild and crazy happenings she was experiencing.

Out of habit, I rose early the next morning and made breakfast. While we ate, we decided to spend our day around the pool. It was a little more convenient. Something to eat was just a few steps away, we had a bathroom if we needed one, and if someone had too much sun, they could go inside the house.

I lay upon a lounge chair by the pool and checked my phone, nearly 9:00.

"Dad! Come quick!" My brother's command sounded urgent. I went inside and discovered he was staring at the TV. He was sitting forward with his forearms resting on his thighs.

I sat on the arm of the couch where he sat mesmerized by the scene unfolding on the screen. "What's going on?"

Dad walked into the room.

My brother looked over his shoulder at me. "I'm watching the Boston Marathon and two bombs just went off."

The cameraman, transfixed by the panic, chaos, and blood, lots of blood, steadied the camera before scanned the roadside. People were scurrying everywhere like carpenter ants when their nest is discovered. Some were running away, others were running to help the injured. I could hardly believe what I was seeing.

"How terrible? Who would do such a thing?" Two people lifted a man into a wheelchair. The helpers. I watched the helpers. Mr. Rodger's quote came to mind, "When I was a boy and I would see scary things in the news, my mother would say to me, 'Look for the helpers. You will always find people who are helping.'" There they were, the helpers, lending a hand wherever needed. They were giving comfort, signaling for medical attention, and carrying the wounded to awaiting ambulances. It was hard to believe what we were witnessing.

Dad sighed. "God bless them."

I said a prayer for those who had died, the injured, and the helpers. I didn't want to watch the tragedy any longer. I returned to my lounge chair and selected a song to play on my cell phone hoping to distract my mind.

*   *   *

I turned to my spirit guide.

"I thought you said she would understand, that the dream would improve our communication. She didn't make the connection."

"*In time.*"

*   *   *

Our day was spent relaxing by the pool with dinner at our favorite restaurant for seafood.

Even though the news on TV and the internet was dominated by the bombing for the week, we enjoyed the remainder of our vacation. After all, it was an opportunity for all of us to relax. It would probably be the last spring break we would spend together as a family. Once I was in college, I assumed my break schedule would be different from my brother's high school schedule. I savored each moment with them, took plenty of pictures, and was thankful for this time together.

The week's end came faster than I wanted. Early Saturday morning we were stripping beds, tidying up the house, and loading our luggage and ourselves in the rental car.

After a smooth flight northward, we were home. Grandma had watched Spooky while we were away. Even though she'd taken good care of him, he looked thin. I began the laundry while Dad went grocery shopping. Even though our trip had been nice, I was ready to finish my last marking period and graduate from high school.

Back To Reality

Many of the students had bronze suntans from their southern vacation. As I walked to my locker, I passed a pair of girls comparing arms to see who had the darkest tan. It was easy to tell who had stayed home for spring break. They were pasty white.

I saw my friend at my locker. Her face was sunburned. She had gone with a group of cheerleaders and sent an occasional text with updates, but I was certain she had more juicy details she was eager to tell me.

"Hey, did you have a good break?" I selected my first-hour book and folder.

She bubbled with excitement as I shut the locker and we walked to class.

"Oh, you have to hear this." She went into an animated detail about who'd hooked up with whom, those who'd been stone drunk, and the partying into the wee hours of the morning. In a way, I felt sorry for some of the people who'd made total fools of themselves, especially some who'd been so drunk that they'd ended up in bed with someone for the night or slept in a bathtub. How embarrassing. Unfortunately, it would be how fellow classmates would remember them after graduation. I was eager to change the topic.

"Can you believe what happened in Boston?"

My friend had a strange look on her face.

"You act surprised. Silly, you told me about the bombing before we left for vacation." She entered the classroom as her reply caused me to halt my steps just outside the door.

I stood frozen recalling the dream; the pavement, tall buildings, two explosions, and the people. The dream was a depiction of the event, right down to the smallest detail. The haunting images of the injured and dead played in my mind like a video and the helpers. *Always remember the helpers.* I had been shown the tragedy before it happened, the future, but had failed to make the connection to my dream. Why? How? Was it a coincidence? *Highly doubtful.* Was it a warning? But why me?

Mom? She wasn't in the dream and would have little reason to warn me about a bombing in Boston, where I was out of harm's way. Was the message to warn others? But I did not know the city. It could have been any city anywhere.

My shoulder was bumped by someone going into the room, and it brought me back to reality. The tardy bell rang as I entered the classroom and sat in my assigned seat. I wanted the haunting images of the tragedy to leave my mind.

Closing A Chapter

I was accepted to every college I applied. Preferring to attend an in-state university, I ruled out the out of state options. Carefully weighing the proximity to home, scholarships awarded, and the number of credits I would receive for my advanced placement classes would determine which university I attended.

I played varsity soccer in the spring. It was strange seeing Mom's usual spot in the stands empty. Dad's work schedule limited the number of games he could attend, but I was thankful when he could be there to cheer me on.

I'd managed to visit the stable at least once a month since Mom's death and ride her horse. The stablemaster assured me the horse was in good hands and veterans were responding well during their therapy. The charity was subsiding his boarding costs, which was nice to know he would have a permanent stable.

Prom was in the next few weeks. I could see little reason for attending such an expensive dance. Many had dates. I hadn't been asked and doubted I would accept even if I was. My friend wasn't asked either. So, we decided we would purchase gowns at the bridal shop, hopefully on clearance, get gussied up, and go out for dinner.

We spent a Saturday morning shopping and were able to find dresses for a good price. Mine would have to be altered. Since I knew little about sewing, I hoped either Grandma or my elderly neighbor could do the alterations.

While we ate a late lunch before I had to go to work, we made appointments to get our hair and nails done and also reservations for dinner.

The day of the prom, Dad took plenty of pictures of the two of us looking our best. We received a lot of compliments from strangers while at a local restaurant. Afterward, we went to my friend's house for a bonfire. I told Dad I was spending the night, so he had little reason to worry, but I sent him a reassuring text letting him know I was fine.

With only a week left of school, it was difficult attending the awards banquet without Mom. I wished she was there to share in my success. Each time my name was called to walk onto the stage and receive an award or scholarship, I looked to Dad's smiling face as he applauded. My brother, who willingly attended the ceremony, applauded as well.

*   *   *

I placed myself in the empty seat next to my husband.

"Well done, Elizabeth. I'm so proud of you." I clapped my hands, knowing the sound would not be heard.

*   *   *

The day was sunny and bright for my commencement. Unfortunately, it was quite humid and warm as everyone sat in the bleachers of the gym for the ceremony. I was able to get through it without shedding a tear. How I wished Mom was there to see this milestone. Dad snapped pictures as I hugged my friends farewell. Except for an occasional text or online chat, it was sad knowing our paths may never cross again. Grandma offered to take a picture of my brother, Dad, and me holding my diploma. I took one with her as well. After commencement, we stopped by our favorite ice cream shop. It was the perfect way to celebrate my educational success.

My open house was the following Saturday. Thank goodness the weather cooperated, and it wasn't as hot as my commencement. Guests sat at the tables and chairs under a rented tent. A long rectangle table contained various dishes of food for the guests to enjoy. Even though Mom and I had planned most of the details, Grandma insisted on helping. I didn't mind, especially since she was a very good cook.

As I watched Grandma replenish serving dishes and tidy, it dawned on me that she was the only grandparent I had. Grandpa had died several years ago, as had Dad's parents. In a way, I was thankful she was there to support my family. She did, however, like to create drama, but I just tried to ignore it. When she would gossip about someone, I would redirect our conversation to something she liked to talk about. I had three go-to options: her health, her cats, and her church activities.

*   *   *

I sighed.

"I wish I could let her know I'm here."

My spirit guided nodded toward a bouquet of colorful balloons on one of the tables.

I smiled in understanding.

"I think I will choose the red one, to represent my love for her."

*   *   *

FROM BEYOND THE GRAVE

As I sat at a table visiting with the neighbor, a red balloon escaped from the centerpiece bouquet on a food table. It brought conversations to a halt as it floated from table to table as if being guided by an invisible thread until it stopped before me. I clasped the dangling ribbon in my hand and looked to the bright red balloon before scanning everyone staring at me. In my heart, I knew Mom was there handing me the balloon. I looked down at the ground. Nestled within the green grass, was a white feather. I picked it up and rose from my seat. Needing a moment to myself, I went to my room and shut the door, added the feather to the vase, and let the tears I had kept in check over the past month fall as I sat on the bed.

"Thank you, Mom. This is the best present ever."

The following month I attended my college orientation. It was interesting, exciting, and scary at the same time. The campus was impressive, but after selecting my classes and noting where they were held, I was a little concerned about having to walk the distance between them and hoped I would be able to arrive at each class on time. My dorm request was granted. I was able to tour it and peek inside a room. It was surprisingly small. I didn't know who my roommate would be, but I hoped we could manage the confined space together. Upon Mom's recommendation, I was going in blind. She had heard of cases where high school friends roomed together, and by the end of the first semester, they disliked each other. I hoped my roommate and I would get along well, and we would remain roommates during our entire time at college.

Even though I had saved money from my job, I decided to do work study. It would be nice to have a little extra cash and not have to depend on Dad to transfer money into my account.

Once home from orientation by mid-afternoon, I made a list of items I wanted to take to college, gathered boxes from the basement, and began filling them. A little premature, but I was excited, yet apprehensive, to experience college life. Part of my concern was leaving the responsibility of the household to Dad and my brother. They would have to take over the laundry, cooking, grocery shopping, and cleaning. Would I come home at semester break to find the house a complete and utter disaster?

Unable to think of anything else to add to the list, I donned my garden gloves and tidied Mom's flower garden. I had to pat myself on the back; it was looking pretty good. Even our neighbor complimented my progress. She had taught me well.

I cooked chicken on the grill for dinner. It was just Dad and me, but I prepared extra for when my brother arrived after work. With it being such a lovely day, we ate outside on the deck.

Dad cut into his chicken.

"Not much longer and you'll be off to college."

"In a way I'm excited, but in another way, I'm scared. I don't know what to expect. Will there be a lot of homework? Will

I like my roommate?" I sighed. "I worry about you too. Do you even know how to cook?"

Dad looked at me with a smirk on his face. "Cook? Sure. I make a wicked peanut butter and jelly sandwich. Mac and cheese from a box can't be too difficult. But what I make best are reservations at a restaurant."

I had to laugh.

"Who's going to clean the house?" I pressed for my next concern. "I don't want to come home at break and work my butt off to get it back in order. Oh, and someone has to clean the cat box too."

He tried to be serious. "I can keep a tidy house."

I gave him a look of disbelief as I tilted my head to the side and raised my eyebrows upward.

He sighed. "If nothing else, I'll get a cleaning service to come in twice a month."

It would have been nice if we had one now instead of me cleaning the house all by myself. I refocused. "Then do me a favor: please put away anything valuable before you let anyone into the house."

"The cleaning companies are insured. If anything happens, they replace it."

"Yes, but once it is gone, it is gone. I would hate to have something of Mom's disappear. So, promise?"

"I promise."

"What about Mom's garden? It needs to have the plants trimmed after a frost."

"Maybe I can ask our neighbor to maintain it now that you have it in good shape, or hire a landscape company. It'll be fine." He picked up his dirty dishes. "Thanks for dinner." He went inside the house.

I sat on the deck and relaxed for a moment. I wasn't ready to do the dishes and put the leftovers away just yet. So much was going through my mind. I wanted to ensure everything was taken care of before I left for college. Maybe going away was going to be more difficult than I thought.

I assumed my classes and studying would occupy most of my time, but would it be too much for me to handle? I hoped to make new friends, and maybe join a club or organization too. I would call home at least once a week, probably on the weekend, to see if all was well and the house was still standing. I looked at my dirty dishes on the table and sighed.

On second thoughts, it would be nice to get away from my responsibilities here. Since I would be eating in the cafeteria, I wouldn't have to do the dishes or cooking. Then there was my laundry, but only mine. Oh, I'd forgotten to add my change jar to the list. I had saved quarters knowing I would need them for the washer and dryer at the end of the hallway in my dorm. I hoped my roommate wasn't a slob. The last thing I wanted was to pick up after someone else. Maybe we would set up a cleaning schedule. Thankfully, the bathroom was communal, and a college employee maintained it.

I sighed, rose, and began gathering the dishes from the table. It took several trips, but I managed to get the job done.

With the kitchen cleaned and food put away, I retreated to my room, packed a few more items for college, and checked them off my list.

Faced with the major change in my life, the unknown, I guessed I would handle each situation the best I could. I looked at the picture of Mom.

"I wish you were here to tell me everything is going to be all right."

Reassurance And Warnings

As I drifted off to sleep, I saw a flash of a picture in my mind. The background was orange with yellow streaks at a focal point that looked like someone had just entered warp speed. There were bold black letters, "MY SON 444" and for some reason, I knew it referred to Philippians.

I opened my eyes. *What did I just see?* *Was this a message from Mom?* "MY SON" or from God himself.

I turned on my lamp. *Where is my bible?* It had been ages since I had seen it. I had received it as first communion present from Grandma when I was in second grade. I got out of bed and went to my closet. Scanning the top shelf filled with boxes and mentally checking each one off, I knew it wasn't in any of them. I searched through the drawer and cupboard in the TV stand, but it wasn't there either. I went to my nightstand and opened the drawer.

"Boy, there is a lot of junk in here." I shifted things back and forth until I spied the white binding and gold lettering. Since I rarely opened the book, I had to flip through the pages. Was Philippians in the Old Testament or New Testament? I finally found it toward the end of the New Testament. Assuming I needed to go to Chapter 4, I turned to it. I scanned for Verse 4. *I guess the last four means I should read for four verses.* I began to read.

"**Joy and Peace**.4 Rejoice in the Lord always! I say it again. Rejoice! 5* Everyone should see how unselfish you are. The Lord is near. 6* Dismiss all anxiety from your minds. Present your needs to God in every form of prayer and in petitions full of gratitude. 7* Then God's own peace, which is beyond all understanding, will stand guard over your hearts and minds, in Christ Jesus."

The words were comforting. A calmness settled within me as I exhaled. Apparently, my worries were heard. I reread the passage again before setting the Bible on my nightstand with the intention of adding it to one of the boxes. I scanned the stack of boxes filled with the essential items I needed while away from home.

Once home for Christmas break, I planned to return to my job. At least that was my plan. I would need to ensure it was fine with my manager. With so much on my mind, sleep eluded me as I tossed and turned most of the night.

*   *   *

Dismayed, I knew Elizabeth had received a message, but it wasn't from me.

My spirit guide stepped beside me.

"*He wanted to reassure her that all would be well.*"

"I am familiar with the passage and am pleased she read it." I sighed as I looked at my spirit guide. "The danger is drawing near." A vision from Him appeared in my mind. "It is important that I warn her once again and hope she makes the connection."

My spirit guide nodded in agreement.

I stood next to her bed and concentrated.

~

I was traveling westward, toward California. I knew I was in the middle of nowhere. A desert was close by, or maybe I was in a desert. I turned northward and found myself in the center of the road, the main street, which was five lanes wide. It didn't make sense. I thought I would discover a ghost town with a dirt street of some sorts. Here I stood on the dotted line of a blacktop street that was five lanes wide. A motorcycle with a man passed by my right side and went into town. I stared at the man. He had black hair.

~

I opened my eyes, laid in bed, and tried to recall the dream's details.

Was it another warning? I wasn't certain where the city was or if it even existed. And who was the man on the motorcycle?

Spooky tried to jump onto my bed, his paws reaching for the edge of my mattress, but he tumbled down to the floor. I pulled back the covers and got out of bed.

"Are you OK?" I picked him up. "You're getting old, Spooky. Fourteen? Fifteen?" I stroked his fur. I looked at my alarm clock. I had two hours until I had to be at work. "Let's see if I can find something in the refrigerator for you to eat."

*   *   *

Spooky reminded me of our past pet.

"Where is Thomas?" I recalled seeing him right after I had died, but had not seen him since I returned.

"*He has moved on. But rest assured, he is fine.*"

"Moved on?"

"*Many spirits travel about this world through portals. He may have discovered one and decided to explore it.*"

"Is there one is the house?"

"*Perhaps, or he may have returned home.*"

He looked to me with a slight grin. Was he waiting for me to discover the portal myself? I would just as soon stay close to my family, for now.

Legally An Adult

My eighteenth birthday, another milestone, but one of significant importance. Like many other birthdays, we would celebrate it by going out to dinner. Idle while working the morning shift, I reviewed my choice of restaurants for my birthday meal. Since I had a craving for the renowned mac and cheese rated third most delicious in our state, I chose the old fire hall restaurant in town.

After the waitress took our order, we held our glasses high and toasted to my good health and future endeavors. Dad placed his glass of beer on the brown paper covered table.

"I received an email today detailing my family's annual meeting. Looks like I'm going to Las Vegas this year."

My brother swallowed before speaking, a rarity.

"Do we get to go?"

"No, it's just for me and my siblings, family estate business."

Since his parents' deaths, Dad and his siblings upheld their promise to meet once a year and distribute a portion of the estate. The annual family meeting was usually held in autumn. I glanced at my brother before looking to Dad.

"When are you going?" I assumed I would be away at college, which would leave my brother home alone. He would probably end up at Grandma's house.

"The third week of September. Probably for a long weekend."

My brother seized the opportunity.

"Do I get to stay home alone? I'll be a junior and have my own car to get around."

"We'll make that decision when the time comes. If need be, we can ask your sister to come home for the weekend." A smirk appeared on Dad's face. "Or we can always have Grandma stay with you or you with her."

My brother's eyes widened. He quickly thought of a third option. "Or I can stay at a friend's house and come home each day to feed the cat."

Quick thinking. I looked at him before taking a drink of my ice water.

Dad reiterated. "We shall see." He placed his hands in his lap as the waitress set his dinner before him.

My mac and cheese, heaven on a plate. I broke through the toasted, crusted cheese with my fork and watched the steam escape. Selecting a few of the penne pasta coated with cheesy goodness, I blew on them hoping they would cool quickly.

I watched as Dad bit into his gigantic cheeseburger. Should I tell him about my recent dream? Would he think I'm crazy? Am I crazy? *Maybe another time.*

I remembered Mom saying I had 'the gift', that my great-grandmother had passed it on to me. Now that I was a year older, were my abilities becoming stronger, or was I becoming more aware of them? Since Mom's death, the dreams had occurred more frequently. Was it a coincidence?

While surfing the internet later that night, I came across an article about the discovery of a terrorist magazine printed in English. The article indicated possible terrorist targets: military bases, military recruiting facilities, military schools, and Las Vegas. I stopped breathing for a moment. *Las Vegas.* That was where Dad and his family were planning their meeting. My heart raced, and my palms began to sweat.

I left my room and went to the family room where Dad was watching TV with my brother.

"Dad, I need to tell you something and I need you to listen to me." I crossed my arms over my chest as I stood between him and the TV.

Perhaps he recognized the serious tone in my voice. He pressed pause on the remote control.

"Hey!" My brother objected to the interruption.

I glared at him.

"This will just take a minute and then you can get back to your movie." I looked at Dad. "You know how you and your family are supposed to go to Las Vegas in September."

"Yes."

"Well, I don't think you should go."

"Why?"

"I know this sounds silly, but I've been experiencing a lot of dreams lately. Some of them have come true. For instance, before we went on spring break, one of my dreams foretold the Boston Marathon bombing. I didn't even make the connection between my dream and the catastrophe until my friend at school pointed it out to me."

Dad stared at me as if I was crazy.

I placed my fisted hands upon my hips. "It's true."

He sighed. "Go on."

I had the feeling he was humoring me, but I continued.

"I had another dream recently. In the dream, I was traveling west toward California. I knew I was in the middle of nowhere, near or in a desert. I turned north and found myself standing on the main street that was five lanes wide. I couldn't understand how a town in the middle of nowhere could have such a large main street. As I stood there, a man on a motorcycle passed by me and drove into the town."

"OK." He indicated he was following my train of thought.

I continued. "Well, I was just on the internet and discovered a post that terrorists who are lone wolves are encouraged to attack military schools, bases, schools, and get this, Las Vegas."

My brother interjected. "So, you think this dream indicates that if Dad goes to Las Vegas, he will get killed?" He smirked, conveying his disbelief.

"That's what I am saying."

He laughed. "That's crap. Anyways, we are north of Las Vegas, so how are you supposed to turn north to go into a city that is south of us?"

"I don't know. I've never been there. All I can tell you is what I saw in the dream." I looked back at Dad. "Seriously Dad, I really think something bad is going to happen to you."

"I'm not close with my family, you know that. I'm the black sheep. But this is a promise I made to Grandma and Grandpa before they passed away. I'm obligated to go, even though I have yet to buy my plane ticket."

Ticket. The word brought the other dream to the forefront of my mind.

"Ticket. This is the first time all four of you in your family will be purchasing a ticket since Mom died. The other dream predicted this as well. Think about it, Dad, please."

"I will." He dismissed me by pointing the remote toward the TV, pushing the button, and the movie began to play.

I went to my room. Since I had never been to Las Vegas, I needed more information. I got on the internet and brought up a map of Las Vegas. I zeroed in on the airport. What did I discover? To leave the airport, one must drive west toward California and then turn north onto the main street. I searched for a picture of the city. Low and behold a photograph appeared of the main street. I counted the lanes in the road. There were five of them. And Las Vegas is in or near a desert too. I went back to the family room.

"Dad." I interrupted his viewing of the movie again.

He put it on pause.

"Yes." His reply tinted with irritation.

"I just brought up the map of Las Vegas on my laptop and discovered when you fly into the city and exit the airport, you travel west toward California and then turn north onto the main street. After bringing up a picture of the city, I counted the lanes on the main street. There are five. Five of them." I emphasized my point while holding up my hand with my fingers spread wide. "How did I know that when I have never been to Las Vegas?"

Both Dad and my brother stared at me in disbelief.

Fisting my hands by my sides, a sternness crept into my voice. "All I have to say is, if you insist on going to Las Vegas, you get your affairs in order. I want your will updated, that is if you even have one, and I need you to go over your finances with me before I go to college. I need to know what bills need to be paid and when." I left the room before he could see the welling tears spill from my eyes and my entire body shaking with fear. I returned to my computer to look up the meaning of the color of the tickets. I discovered black meant death and red represented blood or love. *Oh, this is not good.* The dreams appeared to be connected to his travel plans. How was I going to be able to concentrate in school knowing he would be going there and could possibly die?

I could feel an impending doom settle within my heart. I knew if Dad went to Las Vegas he would die. My sleep was restless. I woke several times during the night, glanced at my alarm clock, and tossed and turned before finding a comfortable position to fall asleep.

*　　　　*　　　　*

Being on the nonphysical side, watching those I love, was a helpless feeling. Yet the insight of what they would face was a privilege. With the need to justify my thoughts, I turned to my spirit guide.

"Even though we did not get along while I was alive, I do not wish her injury. She leads a busy lifestyle for one her age. It would be unfair if she could not continue to do so."

"*If she is not warned, there is a possibility she will not survive.*"

"My only hope is to go through Elizabeth, even though she is burdened with so much already." I placed a white feather upon her nightstand and looked at my beautiful daughter.

~

I was talking to Grandma on the phone as she walked from her dining room, opened the door, and stepped into her 2-car garage. It was strange. I could see through her eyes as if my body was inside of her body. Her garage door was open, and the sun was shining. There was a strange man standing on the driveway near the far corner of the garage. He stared at me, rather Grandma. He looked like he was waiting for her, stalking her, constantly lurking nearby. His pants resembled dirty tan Dockers. His shirt was a worn red and brown plaid flannel. He resembled a scarecrow, he was so very thin. His hair looked like greasy brown straw on each side of his emaciated face. His complexion was a deathly olive gray. He seemed severely dehydrated, like he was ill, or even had been dead for a few weeks. The word 'creepy' kept repeating in my mind as he walked across the opening of the garage, staring at us with each step he took, just staring.

~

My alarm rang pulling me from the dream. I shut off the incessant beeping, picked up the feather, and lay still for a moment, twirling the plumage between my thumb and forefinger. *Thanks, Mom.* I put the feather in the vase, opened the drawer in my nightstand, and took out a spiral notebook and pen. I thought it would be a good idea to start journaling my dreams, visions, or whatever they were. I described each dream in detail and estimated the date I experienced it. I wrote today's date at the top of the next page and paused. The anniversary of Mom's death. Checking the time, I jotted down the detail of my latest dream quickly, fed the cat, and rushed to get ready for work.

The image of the creepy man gnawed at my conscious. I got in my car, called Grandma, and backed out of the driveway.

"Hello, you."

Dang caller ID. Her usual greeting. She thought she was being funny but wasn't.

"Grandma, I need..." I was interrupted.

"Well, I haven't heard from you in a long time."

"I know. I've been busy with work and getting ready for college. I don't have long to talk because I'm on my way to work."

"You shouldn't be talking on your cell while driving."

"That's texting, Grandma. This is important, so please listen." No reply, so I continued. "I had a dream that I was talking to you on the phone. You were in your dining room and went into your garage. The garage door was open. There was a creepy man standing just outside your garage on the driveway. He walked across the garage door opening. He was creepy, very creepy. He looked like a scarecrow. His face was gaunt, and he was staring at you. You need to be careful." I conveyed my warning as I turned into the parking lot and parked my car.

"I'll be careful. I think it may be a good idea to go to church, get some holy water, and sprinkle it on the ground at the base of the garage door. I think I'll do that to my door and windows too."

I didn't have time for her rambling, nor did I want to listen to it.

"I'm at work, so I'll let you go. Bye."

Her voice echoed as I pulled my cell away from my ear.

"Bye, love ya."

I ended the call and stuffed my phone in my pocket, exhaled, and entered the building for work.

I thought about the anniversary of Mom's death throughout the day. After work, I went to the grocery store, purchased an inexpensive bouquet of flowers, and drove to the cemetery. After parking my car, I found her grave and stood for a moment. It was so quiet, deathly quiet. I knelt and placed the flowers on the edge of the granite.

"Hi, Mom. I know that you aren't here, that you are in a peaceful place. I can't believe it has been a year already. A year of firsts without you; birthdays, holidays, vacations, and we missed you at all of them." Tears pooled in my eyes. "I'm doing my best and trying to make good decisions without your advice, but I'm certain you already know that. I think I understand some of the dreams that I have had, and I'm torn between going away or staying home to attend college. I feel as if I'm needed here, at home where I can continue to work while attending classes, maybe even take some online. That way I can help maintain the house and watch over everything else." I sighed as I wiped away a tear from my cheek. "I love and miss you and wish you were here so I could talk to you." I kissed the palm of my hand and touched it to her name on the tombstone before rising. "Bye Mom."

Putting The Pieces Together

After dinner, I reread my journal. Two of my dreams appeared to fit together like a puzzle, warning of the disastrous future my family would face if Dad went to Las Vegas. Drawing my conclusion, my insides quivered as I fought back tears. *Worried? Yes, very.* I was determined to convince him to not go on the trip. If he refused to listen to reason, my only recourse was to ensure his will was up to date, that bills were organized with due dates noted, that information for bank accounts and life insurance policy were readily available, and whatever else we should do if the inevitable should happen had been covered. I assumed he would refuse to heed my warning and defer compiling the information and his decision to another time.

Spooky meowed. I looked down to my bedroom floor to see his big blue eyes staring up at me. Setting my journal on my nightstand, I reached over the side of my bed and I picked him up.

"Hi, buddy." I stroked his fur before shutting off my lamp and snuggling him closely as I drifted off to sleep.

~

I was standing in Grandma's garage. The creepy guy walked past the open garage door again. His clothing was the same, but he looked different this time. His eyes were missing. It was as if they had been removed, gouged out, and blood was running down his cheeks from his empty eye sockets. He stared at me and kept staring until he disappeared on the other side of the garage.

~

When I woke, the dream made me shudder. The warning had intensified, going from bad to worse. I called Grandma.

"Hi Grandma, it's me again."

"Well, hello me."

As usual, her greeting aggravated me.

"I had the same dream again, but the creepy guy's eyes were gouged out and blood was dripping from his eye sockets onto his cheeks. He's creepy, very creepy."

"Well, I know how you have the gift and I took your last phone call seriously. I did as I said I would. I went to church and took an empty water bottle with me. I filled it with holy water and drizzled across the opening of my garage. It's about as much protection I can hope for other than praying."

"OK. Just be vigilant. I think he is still there. It's like he is waiting or stalking you or something." I got out of bed and headed toward the bathroom.

"I will."

She started to babble about someone, I assumed, she knew from church, but I simply told her I had to begin my day and had to go. I didn't want to hear about her church gossip.

Three days later, on my way home from work, my cell rang as I pulled in the driveway. I cringed when I saw her name on the caller ID.

"Hello, Grandma."

"Well, hello to you too."

"What's up?"

"I just called to tell you something. I had a friend over and we were in the garage. We needed to get my watering can. For some reason, it was on a high shelf. I'm not quite certain how it got up there. I usually keep it on a lower shelf. Anyway, he was going to get on my old wooden stepladder, but I'm more agile than he is, so I insisted I climb up to get it. I went up to the third step and it broke when I put my full weight on it. I started falling. On my way down to the cement floor, I prayed 'not my back'. Somehow, I rotated in the air and landed on my side. I swear, if I would have landed on my back, I would have hit my head on the concrete and could have seriously injured myself, maybe even died. I landed with a thud. I'm bruised quite badly, but I am OK."

"Oh, that's terrible, but I'm glad you're fine."

"Since my fall, I've thought about the two dreams quite a bit. I think that creepy man you saw was the angel of death. I think I cheated death."

"I'm doubtful I saw death. I don't know. Well maybe. He was quite creepy."

"I think he was the angel of death and your dreams were warnings. I hope he is gone for good."

"Me too. Let's hope I don't have any more dreams about him, but if I do, at least we know something bad could happen."

"Yes."

There was a moment of silence between us. Grandma spoke first. "Well, I know you're busy, but come and see me some time when you're not."

"I will." I lied. Being in her company was never an easy thing for me to do. "I'm glad you are all right. Goodbye."

"Bye-bye."

My dreams, wherever they come from, seemed to occur for a reason. It was reassuring to have someone believe in them, even if it was Grandma. I did wonder though, had her faith and the holy water protected her? I shut my car door and turned to see Dad's car pull in the driveway.

I was leaving for college next week. How was I going to convince him not to go to Las Vegas?

Preparations Complete

I scanned the boxes and bags lined up by my bedroom door. I hoped I had not forgotten anything. If I had, I could always come home on a weekend to get it or have Dad send it in the mail.

Dad had my car checked by our mechanic to ensure it was sound for the two-hour commute and would withstand the challenge of winter driving. It was one less thing I had to worry about as well.

I was leaving in the morning. I had said my farewells at work and received a bonus from my boss, who insisted I return to work during semester breaks and next summer. It was nice to have a guaranteed job waiting for me. However, I had yet to decide if I was returning home for the summer. I could either stay on campus to attend classes or return to my job and take classes online.

My last night at home, and Dad insisted we go out to dinner. Even my brother made a point to join us. I was hesitant to bring up the subject, but I needed to convince Dad not to go to Las Vegas. Since he is an eleventh-hour type of guy, I assumed he had yet to book his flight.

We went to a restaurant in town. After the waiter took our order, Dad sighed before looking toward me.

"Are you excited for tomorrow?" He tried to smile.

I wondered if he was thinking about my first day of school when he'd walked me to kindergarten, and how time had passed so quickly. I wasn't his little girl any more. The time had come for him to let me go and be on my own.

"Yes, and no. I feel as if I should stay here and attend college locally."

"No. Us men will hold down the fort until you return, that's if it's still standing." He smiled teasingly and winked at my brother before taking a sip of his beer.

"We got everything under control, Sis."

Dad's sense of humor made me smile. My brother's response was anything but reassuring. I displayed a not so confident scowl.

"It'll be strange to be away until Christmas. This is a big change for me, being away from home for so long, but I think I'm ready for it."

Dad picked up his beer.

"I think you'll do just fine. And I'm only a phone call away."

OK, now for the tough question. My hands began to tremble at the thought of breaching the subject.

"And I don't need the distraction of worrying about you going to Las Vegas." I began. "I still think something bad is going to happen there."

Dad took a sip of his beer and placed it back on the table. "It was just a dream."

"And some of my dreams have come true." I was determined to persuade him, to see my point of view. "I believe there is a connection between the two dreams. Remember me telling you about the tickets Mom handed you when her arm came through the mirror on the wall?"

"Yes."

"I think Mom may be trying to warn us. When you and your family, all four of you, purchase a ticket, something bad is going to happen. Think about it. It makes sense." I paused letting what I said sink in. "I looked up the meaning of colors in a dream. Black represents death and red stands for blood or love. I believe the second dream with the lone motorcycle rider has to do with Las Vegas too. Don't go, Dad."

"I'd be the only one in my family not attending. I would never hear the end of it if I don't go."

"It's better than dying and leaving us alone." I clenched my teeth, trying to keep my emotions in check, and took a deep breath. "Besides, you have yet to make a will and discuss finances with me." I looked at my brother, who was distracted by his cellphone. "Where would we be if something should happen to you?" It was a poor attempt at using guilt.

When Mom had died, Dad had told me they didn't have a will and he needed to draw up one. He had yet to take the time to do so. Sometimes I thought by avoiding doing so, he wouldn't have to admit he would die some day. Silly. We would all die. I thought everyone should focus on living a full life and admire how a person lived instead of how they died.

Dad looked toward the approaching waiter carrying a tray of food.

"I'll make my decision next week."

"Seriously, you're going to let me go away to college without knowing your decision?" My insides were shaking.

"I need to discuss this with my family first."

I stared at him. *Goodness sake get a spine.* The waiter set my plate of food before me. End of discussion for now.

Dad changed the subject. He began his fatherly talk on all the dos and don'ts of being on my own at college. Much of it I knew, but I think it made him feel better repeating it for the umpteenth time. He paused to take a bite of his steak, giving me time to look at my brother with an 'I've heard this before' kind of look. He smirked.

FROM BEYOND THE GRAVE

Stuffing the last bite into my mouth, I pushed my plate away. Probably my last good meal for a while. I had been forewarned about the high-carb food and the freshman fifteen I would probably pack onto my hips. I vowed to make healthy choices and avoid eating late at night. I planned to exercise daily, or as much as my schedule allowed. Walking to classes would help too.

As I tucked myself into bed, Dad peeked his head into my room. "Since I'll be at work when you leave for college, good luck tomorrow." He entered my bedroom and I got out of bed and wrapped my arms around his neck as he hugged me dearly.

"I'll be fine. I love you, Dad. Besides, you're just a phone call, text, or two hours away."

"I know." He chuckled, knowing it was my habit to contact him during a business meeting. His eyes pooled with tears. "Your mother would be so proud of you." He forced a smile.

"I know."

"Well, good night."

"Good night."

He closed the door halfway as he left my room. I shut off my lamp and returned to bed hoping I would sleep well. I had my doubts.

A New Chapter

I smiled as I looked down at the angelic face of my sleeping daughter.

"My husband is right. I am proud of her."

"Yes, her future is promising."

~

I stood in a field, far away from home. The morning air was thick with fog. A horse came from nowhere. It crossed from left to right in front of me, nearly stepping on my toes. Its mane was off-white, blonde, and its coat was deep brown, like dark chocolate. It had thick long blonde hair covering its hooves. It was beautiful, and such an unusual color.

Sitting on its back, was a man. His face was blurred and unrecognizable, as if someone had taken an eraser and smeared it. His beard and hair were long, dark, and a bit wavy. He wore a hat, a plaid tam tipped to the right side of his head. His white shirt with billowing long sleeves fitted tightly around his wrists. He wore a kilt with his tartan thrown over his left shoulder, held in place with a silver brooch. The wool was a plaid of deep forest green and black with thin white stripes. His legs were bare except for the knee-high stocking that peeked over the top of his tall black boots.

He pulled on the horse's reins, drawing it to a stop. The horse remined still as the man stared down at me. I could only assume he was staring at me since I couldn't see his eyes. Why was his face obscured? Was his identity a secret? It was as if I knew him, yet I did not. I wasn't afraid, just curious, and I stood my ground. He seemed to be the same. Without a word, he touched his heals to the sides of his horse and continued their journey.

~

I was alone in the house when I rose the next morning. I retrieved my journal from within a box, and jotted down the dream. I shared my scrambled eggs with the cat before showering, dressing for the day, and carrying my bags and boxes to the car.

"All loaded." I closed the trunk.

I went to my room to ensure I had not forgotten anything, even though I had made an extensive list and every item was crossed off, including Mom's sweater. I walked through Dad's bedroom, pausing, and peeked into my brother's bedroom. Spooky lay curled like a snake on the end of his bed, sleeping.

It was strange to walk through the house room by room as if saying goodbye. I closed the garage door, got inside my car, and inserted the key into the ignition. My body jerked, startled by the tapping on my passenger window. It was our neighbor. She smiled as she held up one finger indicating she wanted a moment of my time. I opened the car door and stood.

She came around the front of my car with a rectangle plastic container in her hand.

"I just wanted to wish you good luck and thought you would like some cookies in case the food isn't too good." She winked and displayed a devilish grin.

"That's very sweet of you." I imagined they were homemade molasses cookies, coated in fine white sugar, soft, and chewy inside.

She handed me the container. "I made these fresh this morning. I know they're your favorite."

She took great pride in her baking. Everything made to perfection. I opened the lid and peeked inside.

FROM BEYOND THE GRAVE

"My favorite. Oh, you know me too well. Thank you."

"You're welcome." She waved as she went back to her yard. "Good luck."

"Thank you." I put the cookies on the passenger seat as I got back into my car. I took one last look at the house and my mother's flower garden before turning the key in the ignition. I checked the gas gauge. As expected, Dad had filled my tank. I backed out of the driveway and drove away.

The two hours went by quickly. I sent Dad a text when I arrived on campus. Since I had attended orientation, I found my dorm easily. After checking into the main office and receiving my keys, I went to my room, which was more like a large walk-in closet. My roommate had already moved in and claimed her dresser drawers and one side of our closet. The bottom bunk bed was neatly made with a colorful comforter and decorative pillows. I sighed as I looked at the top bunk. A pair of desks lined one wall with framed photographs displayed on one. After examining the picture, I determined which person in the photographs was most likely my roommate. Wherever the photographs had been taken, the countryside in the background was beautiful.

I went to my car to unload the rest of my bags and looked down at the asphalt as I reached for the handle of the door. Lying there was a white feather. Never passing up the opportunity to add one more to my collection, I reached down and picked it up. *It's reassuring to know you're with me. Thanks,*

Mom. I tucked the feather inside one of the boxes before picking it up.

After several trips, my car was unloaded. I drove it to my assigned parking spot in the lot on the other side of campus. I thought it was ridiculous to have to pay to keep my car on campus. Just another way for the college to make money.

The walk back to my dorm took me through the heart of campus. With classes beginning in two days, the campus buzzed with people unloading their cars, entering and exiting the dorms, and bidding their farewells. Watching a father hug his daughter goodbye made me wish Dad could have come with me and done the same.

The door to my room was open. I assumed my roommate was inside. I took a deep breath. I had heard horror stories of roommates who butted heads and didn't get along. *Please be someone I can tolerate.*

My roommate was sitting at her desk. She looked up from her laptop as I entered.

"Hello, my name is Molly, but you can call me Mol."

I detected a heavy accent in her voice.

"I'm Elizabeth. Where are you from?"

"Ireland. I've already been here a week. I hope you don't mind. I unpacked my things. We can switch drawers or beds if you prefer the ones I chose."

"No, it's fine, I'll just put my things in the other drawers. The top bunk is fine too."

Mol watched as I began to unpack.

"So, this is your freshman year?"

"Excuse me?" Her accent was quite heavy, or maybe she had spoken too quickly for me to understand. It was funny that we both spoke English and yet I couldn't understand what she said.

"Are you a freshman?"

"Yes, and no. I passed all of my advanced high school classes, so academically I'm a sophomore."

We talked and got to know each other while I unpacked. Neither of us had a boyfriend. She seemed nice.

It was lunchtime by the time I finished unpacking, and I placed my sheets, pillow, and blankets on my bed. I would make it later.

The cafeteria was close to our dorm. I felt as if all eyes were upon us as we entered. The guys stared as if we were fresh meat. Heaven forbid I trip and fall or do something foolish. I followed Mol as she explained the different cafeteria stations and what was served at each one. My meal tasted fine, but I looked forward to one of the molasses cookies from my neighbor for dessert.

When we returned to the dorm, I made up my bed and placed Mom's sweater under my pillow. I turned to see Mol with a quizzical look upon her face. Uneasy, I was compelled to explain.

"My mom died just over a year ago. I like to keep her sweater near me when I sleep because it smells like her."

"My mom died a year ago too. Dang cancer."

Ah, something else in common, even though it was something sad. Rather than dwell on what couldn't be changed, I switched topics as I took the container from the shelf on my side of the closet and offered her a cookie.

"I thought I would walk to the bookstore tomorrow to purchase my books. What classes are you taking this semester?" I sat at my desk, turned on my laptop, and brought up my schedule.

We compared classes. Two of our classes were the same. I ventured an idea. "Why don't I buy the book for this class," I pointed to my schedule, "and you buy the book for the other class. We can share them? It'll save us some money."

"Good thinking." She smiled before biting into the cookie.

My Untamed Roommate

Mol insisted we attend a party for the evening.

"Come on. It's a frat party! Everyone goes. It's a kick-off for the coming year."

"Frat?"

"Ya, you know, a fraternity, guys."

"I'm not the partying type. And on top of that, I'm underage."

"Oh, come on. There will be lots of people there. Nearly the entire campus."

I sighed as I nodded my head conceding.

Mol fluffed her brunette hair, touched up her make-up, and changed her shirt.

Wanting to fit into the college lifestyle, I touched up my face and dabbed perfume on each wrist.

We walked to the frat house and stood outside on the sidewalk. I elbowed Mol.

"It's huge. How many guys live here?"

"A lot. Come on. Let's go inside." Mol tugged my arm pulling me down the sidewalk and into the house.

* * *

"What is she doing? I warned her about things like this."

"*She is learning. There are lessons that one must learn for themselves.*"

"Oh, this is bad, very bad." I turned to my spirit guide. "Isn't there anything I can do?"

"*No, we are not to intervene, only observe.*"

"But this could go terribly wrong. Shouldn't I warn her?"

"*No.*"

* * *

There was music blaring, dancing, and people mingling shoulder to shoulder. I stayed close to Mol as she pushed her way to the kitchen where the keg of beer sat in an ice-filled galvanized tub.

FROM BEYOND THE GRAVE

A guy with rust-colored hair held a red Solo cup in his hand while filling it from the tap. He looked toward us.

"Lovely ladies, I think you are in need of a beverage." He handed Mol the filled glass, which in turn she gave to me. I lowered my nose to its rim and inhaled. Repulsive. But I took a sip anyway. It was worse tasting than I imagined, but I sipped it anyway as I peeked over the brim of the cup at the others in the room.

Once Mol had her drink in hand, we wove our way to the large living room. The architecture of the old mansion was magnificent. Its paneled walls of dark-stained wood wainscoting and a Victorian style wallpaper above it brought a coziness to the room. An elegant fireplace was bookended with columns below and above the mantel. A mirror hung above. I wondered how many times it had been broken and replaced over the years. The furniture was leather, but modern. It looked a bit out of place in the historic room, but I imagined antique furniture couldn't withstand the rough treatment its residents would have put it through. The area rug on the hardwood floor had several stains. I watched as a guy backed into a gal, spilling her drink onto the floor. There were built-in bookshelves on each side of the fireplace, displaying trophies, sculptures, photographs, and books.

As I turned around, I found myself alone. Mol had somehow separated from me. I continued to sip my beer as I walked around the room. At least with the cup near my mouth, I didn't have to talk to anyone. I wandered over to the bookshelves and began perusing the items on display.

"What ya looking at?"

Hesitantly, I looked to my left to see a guy leaning his shoulder against the bookcase. He had a thick beard, was of medium height, and had a bulbous belly, as if he could drink an entire keg of beer by himself. I lowered my glass from my mouth.

"I was reading the titles on the books." I looked to my right for Mol. Still no sign of her.

Mr. Disgusting tapped me on my shoulder to get my attention.

"You want to go upstairs and find a bedroom?"

Seriously? Not exactly an inviting pick-up line.

"No, thank you." I turned and walked away. Tipping my cup, I drank the last of my beer and headed back to the kitchen to see if Mol was there. Without thinking, I accepted a second glass with foam spilling over the edge and took a sip. No sign of my roommate as I scanned the kitchen before leaving.

After several more glasses of beer, I needed to find the bathroom. My head felt disconnected from my body and my eyes seemed heavy. I sidestepped, bumping into someone next to me. I wandered down a hallway and seemed to bounce from one side to the other like a ping pong ball. A girl opened a door and stepped into a hallway. I peeked into the room. *Ah, a bathroom.* I entered and locked the door. It took some effort, but I managed to pull down my jeans and sit before I wet myself.

Fumbling with the toilet paper, I managed to dry myself, flush the toilet, and wash my hands. I unlocked the door and stepped into the hallway. I stumbled into the living room. Several people turned and were staring at me. Some were laughing.

Mol rushed toward me.

"Elizabeth, what are you doing?" She reached toward my zipper and yanked away the toilet paper that trailed down the hallway all the way to the bathroom. "We need to get you back to the dorm. Stay here while I say goodbye to someone." I leaned against the wall, watched her turn around, and walk away before hearing a voice coming from behind me.

"Hey babe, how about a kiss?"

Without thinking, I turned toward him, allowed my heavy eyelids to close, and tilted my face upward. His lips were demanding. I responded with more vigor than I thought I had in me.

"All right, we have to go." Mol tugged on my arm, pulling away from whomever I was kissing, and guided me toward the front door. I teetered to one side, bumping into someone.

"Sorry," I heard Mol say before we stepped through the front door and onto the porch where the overflow of the party lingered. A guy stepped in front of us.

"Do you need help getting her home?"

Mol looked to the musclebound guy, probably a football player.

"No thanks, I can manage."

I grabbed the railing and guided myself down the stairs to the sidewalk. Out of earshot of others, I confided my embarrassment.

"Mol, I'm sorry. I guess I drank too much. Sorry you have to babysit me."

"It's fine. There may come a time when you do the same for me."

Disoriented

I opened my eyelids lethargically as my body shook. I looked into the baby blue eyes of a guy leaning over me.

"Are you OK?"

I watched as he stood to his full height. He was tall and broad-shouldered, with dark curly hair. I tried to orientate myself as I scanned the room. I was in the dorm lobby, sitting in a chair, and sleeping? What the hell? How did I end up in the lobby?

"Yes, I'm fine." Still half-asleep, I pushed myself to stand, left the lobby, and headed down the hall toward my room. As I got to the door, I looked back to the end of the hallway. He was standing there watching me. *Creepy*. I opened the door and went inside to find my pillow and blanket on the floor next to the wastepaper basket.

I threw my blanket and pillow onto my bed and climbed in. What happened last night? I remember going to the party, drinking a beer, well, maybe a few? How did I end up sleeping in the lobby?

My head hurt a little, but other than that, I felt fine as I drifted back to sleep.

*   *   *

"At least she made it safely back to her room."

"*Yes, and a lesson possibly learned.*"

"I hope so. There are many who say, 'I'm never doing that again', yet they do."

*   *   *

"Do you want anything from the cafeteria?"

I opened my eyes to see the tiles of the ceiling. My mouth was dry. I looked to my left. Mol was staring at me. Since she was short, she was probably standing on her mattress.

"What time is it?" I reached for my phone, but it wasn't where I normally kept it to charge during the night. *Probably dead.* Still wearing my clothes from yesterday, I pulled my phone out of the back pocket of my jeans and tapped the screen. *Yep, dead all right.*

"It's nearly one o'clock in the afternoon."

"One o'clock? I've never slept this late in my life."

"Well, after the night you had, you needed to sleep it off."

I rolled onto my side toward Mol. "How did I get in the lobby?"

My roommate's eyebrows raised upward. "The lobby?"

"Yes, some guy woke me up this morning. At least I think it was morning. He asked me if I was all right."

"What were you doing there?"

"Apparently sleeping in a chair."

"You must have left our room after I fell asleep. All I know is that I found you with toilet paper wedged in your zipper after you had apparently used the restroom at the party. The dang stuff made a trail from you, down the hall, and into the bathroom. It was quite a sight." She snickered.

"Oh, lovely. I made a complete fool of myself." I rolled back onto my back.

"Oh, that's not all. I had to pull you away from kissing a guy."

I gingerly raised myself onto my elbow, my mouth gaping open, and looked toward her.

"I kissed someone? Who?"

"I don't know who he was, but it looked as if both of you were enjoying it."

"Good lord."

"I brought you back to the room. I couldn't get you into your bed. Besides, if you were going to throw up, I didn't want you puking on me from the top loft."

"So, you put my pillow and blanket on the floor and let me sleep there."

"Yes, along with the wastepaper basket next to you, just in case."

I foggy memory seeped within my mind.

"I vaguely remember using the bathroom during the night. I must have gone to the lobby instead of coming back to our room. This is embarrassing."

"Oh, cheer up. Nothing bad came of it and we had a good time."

"It would be nice if I could remember it though." *I swear I'm never doing something so stupid like that again.*

"So, what would you like to eat?"

"I would prefer a coffee, bagel, and cream cheese, but I doubt the cafeteria is still serving it this late in the day."

"I'll see what they have. Be back soon."

"OK."

I sighed hoping the warm water of a shower would ease the start of my day. I climbed down from my upper bunk and plugged in my phone to charge. With a change in clothing, my toiletry caddy, and towel in hand, I headed toward the bathroom.

FROM BEYOND THE GRAVE

After pulling the curtain shut on the shower cubical, I unzipped my pants and discovered remnants of the toilet paper in my zipper. I shook my head, but soon regretted the pounding ache that ensued.

Once showered, dressed, and with my hair combed straight, I returned to my room to see my roommate sitting at her desk. Mol looked toward me as I entered the open door.

"I brought you grilled cheese and tomato soup."

"Sound great. Thanks." As I put my caddy in the closet, a knock sounded on our open door.

Mol stood abruptly from her chair.

"Well, hello." She glanced at him from head to toe and gave him a flirtatious grin.

I peeked my head around the corner of the closet to see who was standing in the doorway. It was the same guy who had woken me in the lobby, Mr. Blue Eyes. After finding me in the lobby asleep in a chair, I could only imagine his first impression of me. My current state, freshly showered, with wet hair, and no make-up wasn't much of an improvement either.

He looked toward me.

"Hi. I just came by to see if you were OK."

Mol stepped beside me.

"She's fine. Come on it, have a seat." She pulled my chair out from my desk and offered it to him. He politely nodded and sat.

I stared at Mol. I could hardly believe her boldness. I looked back to the guy sitting in my chair.

"I'm sorry, we've not been properly introduced. I'm Elizabeth and this is Molly." I motioned toward my roommate as she turned her desk chair to face him, sat, and stared.

"But you can call me Mol." She smiled.

I had the feeling he didn't quite know what to think of Mol.

"I'm Jasper, Jasper McLean."

"It's nice to meet you Jasper, but as you can see, I'm perfectly fine. I appreciate your concern for my welfare."

Mol jumped into the conversation. "We went to the frat party last night." She cupped her chin with her hand. "I don't recall seeing you there."

I watched as Jasper looked at me, and mentally put together my reason for sleeping in the lobby. He looked back to Mol. "I didn't attend. I try to avoid big campus parties. Being a member of the soccer team, there are too many eyes watching for violators. Athletes can get kicked off a team for drinking."

Still standing, I looked around the room. *We need another place for visitors to sit.* With no other option, I sat on Mol's bed.

Mol couldn't contain herself. She easily carried the conversation for both of us.

"So, soccer team. You mean football, right?"

I went on to explain. "Mol is from Ireland."

Jasper understood her confusion. "Yes, football." He turned to me. "You're both freshmen?"

We looked at each other. Mol spoke first. "I'm a junior. Just came here to continue my education and do some traveling after the school year is finished."

Jasper turned to me.

"I'm a freshman, but technically a sophomore since I earned college credits in high school," I explained.

Mol batted her eyes. "And you, Jasper?"

"I'm a sophomore."

He turned back to me. "Well, I have to go. I just wanted to see if you were OK." Jasper stood and politely returned my chair to its rightful place at my desk.

"Thanks. I'm fine other than a headache."

"Well, being the weekend, you can lay around, drink lots of water, and recover. See you around."

Mol looked up at him from where she was sitting.

"See ya, Jasper."

I watched as he stepped into the hallway. "Bye, Jasper." I looked at Mol's stupidly grinning face.

"Well, Elizabeth, that was nice of him to check on you." She raised her eyebrows teasingly.

"Yes, it was nice of him to do so." I downplayed her romantic implication and took the tomato soup and grilled cheese from the paper bag on my desk. Assuming they were cold, I placed them in the microwave to reheat.

*   *   *

We hovered in the hallway as Jasper passed us with his spirit guide in tow.

"It was difficult watching her go through that learning experience."

"*It was necessary.*"

"How so?" I turned and looked to my spirit guide seeking clarification.

"*Unbeknown to her, the circumstance has brought them together.*"

"Who? Not the guy she kissed?

"*No.*"

"The guy who wanted to take her to the bedroom?"

"*No.*"

I looked down the hallway as Jasper turned the corner and disappeared. The man on horseback wearing a tartan. A Scotsman. McLean. I turned to my spirit guide.

"It's Jasper."

"*Their relationship is preordained, but as you say, not etched in granite.*"

"So, we get to do some 'matchmaking'?"

"*No, we cannot interfere. We can only encourage.*"

"How?"

"*Leave signs such as your feathers for positive thoughts she may have toward him.*"

"What if she does not choose him?"

"*It is a possibility.*"

"Does she know she is to choose him?"

"*Subconsciously, but it has been blocked. It is a matter of her searching within her heart and following the pathway. In truth, he must do the same. They decided to become man and wife in this life before being born. They are what you call soulmates, but there is always the chance of it not happening. As I have stated, it is a choice they must each make.*"

"What if they don't choose to commit to each other?"

"*They may each live a life of solitude or unhappiness.*"

"Let's hope it doesn't come to that. I think it would be rather dismal to grow old by oneself or endure a miserable life." I peeked into the room to see a woman appear in the corner by the ceiling. She looked to me briefly and nodded in acknowledgment. I turned to my spirit guide. "Molly's mother?"

"*Yes, she looks in on her from time to time.*"

I looked down the hallway as a student left her room with her spirit guide following. *One is never alone, never completely alone.*

We Meet Again

After resting for a few hours and drinking several bottles of water from our minifridge, I felt fine. I assumed my headache would subside over time. I wanted to get out of the room. I looked to Mol.

"Let's go to the bookstore."

"Sounds good."

After the short walk across campus, I brought up my schedule on my cellphone, selected my books, and stood in line behind Mol as she purchased her books. My mouth dropped open when the cashier said the total.

"After the semester, you can return your books for cash, but they give you next to nothing for them," a familiar male voice said.

I turned around to see Jasper standing behind me. His hair was wet, and his face flushed.

He grinned. "It's better to buy online or rent them." He held up a textbook for me to see. "Unfortunately, this one wasn't available."

"I'll keep that in mind, thanks." I turned back to the cashier, set my books on the counter, and paid with my debit card.

I stepped to one side and followed Mol while she continued to shop. I looked back at Jasper as he stood at the counter. As if he knew I was looking at him, he glanced toward me and grinned before turning back to the cashier and paying for his book. I had to admit, his dark curly hair and blue eyes were quite a lethal combination, he was very handsome. I was leery though. With his good looks and fit body, I bet he had all kinds of girls chasing after him, and he probably already had a girlfriend. Not that I was interested in him though. Just my first impression.

Mol sighed. "Ready?"

On our way back to the dorm, we stopped and reviewed a campus map. It was the kind that you find in a mall that is labeled 'you are here'. I wanted to refresh my memory of where my classes were located. Out of the corner of my eye, I could see Jasper headed our way. I elbowed my roommate.

"Don't look now, but Jasper is coming this way." I cringed.

She looked toward him. "Oh, he's very cute. Nice smile too. And don't even get me started about his body."

Jasper joined us at the campus map.

Mol smiled as she shifted her books from her right to left hip. "Hello, Jasper. We just stopped to make sure we know where the buildings are for our classes." She flipped her long brunette hair over her shoulder. Was she flirting with him?

Mol took command of the conversation once again, thank goodness. With my schedule on my phone, I turned back to the map and found each building. Groaning internally, I realized I had an 8am class three days a week. Showering in the evening would allow me to sleep in a little while longer in the morning. Unless I had breakfast bars in my room, I would have to allow time to stop at the cafeteria before class. I calculated my alarm time to be 6am for the first day, promising myself to refrain from pressing the snooze button multiple times.

Mol and Jasper started walking back to the dorm. My roommate stopped and looked over her shoulder.

"Elizabeth, are you coming?"

I looked toward them, returned my phone to the back pocket of my jeans, and quickened my steps to catch up to them. The sidewalk was narrow, so I followed behind them and listened to their conversation. They mostly talked about Mol's impression of our campus, country, and living away from home.

Mol continued to grin like a ninny all the way back to our dorm. Jasper resided in our dorm but in the adjacent hallway. He held the door open for us to enter first. We paused at our hallway entrance.

Mol turned toward him. "See you later, Jasper."

Wishful thinking on her part.

"Bye, Mol, Elizabeth." He looked directly at me.

"See ya." I gave him a slight grin before turning down the hallway to our room. My roommate waved goodbye before joining me.

We were halfway to our room when Mol could no longer contain her excitement. "Oh my gosh, he is so cute and so nice."

"You think so?" I turned my key in the lock and opened the door.

"You don't I think so? Are you kidding me? He's handsome."

"Yes, and I bet all of the other girls on campus think he is 'so cute' too. He probably has a girlfriend already."

"He doesn't. I asked. I think he has a thing for you."

"I doubt it. He seems more interested in you than me. He talked with you the entire time."

"That's so he could stay close to you. I know these things. Trust me."

"How do you know these things?"

"I just know."

"I think you're reading too much into it."

I set my books on my desk and began to look through them. I needed to call Dad. The mere thought of his trip to Las Vegas sent tremors of worry through my body. Unable to concentrate, I placed my books on the shelf above my desk and looked toward my roommate.

I hadn't known Mol long, but one thing I had learned, she was more outgoing than me. I'm the kind of person who needs to get to know someone before putting my trust in them. Some would say I'm old fashioned, a little introverted, but it's who I am.

Mol plopped down in her desk chair.

"What shall we do now?" This indicated she was bored.

"Well, it may be a good idea to read the first chapter in each textbook to understand what the professors are talking about."

"I doubt they will assign anything on the first day. More than likely they'll just go over the syllabus."

I checked the time on my phone. I planned to call Dad later tonight. "I'd like to visit the campus library. I might as well get familiar with it since I plan to spend time there in between classes and study."

Mol stood. "Good idea. Let's go."

The building was impressive, three stories high. We entered on the second floor, the main lobby. A woman looked up from the front desk and smiled.

"Can I help you?"

I thought this was a good time as any to inquire about a work-study job. I had taken media services in high school, so I thought working in the library would be a good fit for me.

"Yes, I studied media services for two years while attending high school and I'd like to apply for a work-study job."

She took an application from a tray on the counter behind her and handed it to me. "Just fill this out and turn it into the student center. You should receive a call within the next week or two."

"Thank you."

The library was devoid of students except for a few people sitting at a table. *Maybe a club or organizational meeting.*

We walked up and down the rows of books taking note of what was on each shelf. I paid attention to the location of the topics I may need for research for my classes. There was a partitioned area with cubicles for students who preferred to study alone in a quiet place. Each cubical had a chair, a table, and a computer. Along one wall were small rooms for groups to meet and work on projects. Two of them were larger in size, to accommodate a greater number of people. We took the stairs to the lower and upper levels, which appeared to be the same but contained different genres of books.

We left the library and went to the student center where I filled out the application and turned it in. We toured the ice arena, the gym, and, at the insistence of my roommate, the weight room where she ogled at the men's sweaty bodies.

My stomach grumbled. "Come on, let's get dinner." I grabbed her arm and pulled her away. She complied reluctantly but jabbered about this guy and that one all the way to the cafeteria.

I checked my phone as we entered. I had a text from my brother. He wanted to know if it would be better to boil or microwave the hot dogs for dinner. *Always boil, geez.* I quickly typed my reply and felt two strong hands grab my shoulders, stopping me from bumping into the person in front of me. I looked up to see Jasper.

"Didn't your mom teach you not to text and walk?" His smile conveyed he was joking, but it brought the haunting memory of my mom warning me to never text and drive.

All I could do was stare at him. His smile faded. He glanced at my roommate. I assumed from the expression on her face, he realized he had said something wrong.

"Sorry, apparently I'm not very good at telling jokes."

My roommate decided to lighten the atmosphere. "Why don't you join us for dinner?"

He looked at me. "Would that be all right with you?"

I forced a grin on my face. I didn't want to appear rude. Besides, I'm certain my roommate would enjoy snuggling next to him in a booth.

"Sure."

I got into the chicken stir fry line and glanced to the burger line to see my roommate and Jasper chatting while they waited. I almost laughed out loud at the way my roommate appeared to be flirting, again.

I selected the vegetables for my meal, watched while it was being prepared, and picked up my tray once the bowl of steaming chicken, vegetables, and rice was placed upon it. After getting my drink and visiting the salad bar for fruit, I selected a booth. Moments later, my roommate and Jasper sat across from me.

Even though they did most of the talking throughout the meal, Mol would pause mid-sentence as a guy entered the cafeteria, which was my cue to add a few words to the conversation while she regained her wits about her.

Becoming a habit, we walked back to the dorm together, parting ways in the hallway.

"He is amazing." Mol sighed as we entered our room. "Don't you think so?"

"I don't know. I feel so guarded around him, like I put up walls to barricade myself safely within. Maybe he's not my type."

"Not your type? Are you kidding? He's tall, handsome, well built, a good personality, polite, my goodness, what's not to like?"

"I don't know. Maybe it's a matter of not trusting him. I've never had a boyfriend before."

Mol's mouth dropped open. "Oh my God! You're a virgin!"

I was thankful the door was ajar only slightly, hoping no one had heard her.

"There's nothing wrong with being a virgin. In truth, I would rather be known as a virgin than a slut who can't keep her legs crossed."

"I agree. Sorry, I was just surprised."

"My mother's morals have guided me through life thus far, and I'm pleased with who I am. I've focused on myself to achieve my high school goals. I've gone on a few dates, but that's as far as it went. I've plenty of time for guys later."

Mol sighed. "I hate to be the bearer of news, but now is later. Think about it. If you don't hook up with someone in college, then when? Once employed after graduation, an office romance can get you fired. He's a good guy. Maybe just be friends with him until you can learn to trust him. That way you can get to know him better and judge for yourself."

"I don't know if I want to know him at all. He could turn out to be just one of those guys that uses me for sex and then throws me away. I don't want to be a throw away girl."

"It's a risk we all take in order to know what we can tolerate in a relationship. For now, no sex, just be his friend and get to know if he is trustworthy or not."

I looked at my cellphone. Dad should be home, a good time to call him.

"I'm not nor do I have the time to be interested in Jasper." I rose from my chair. "I'm going to the lobby to make a phone call."

A Call Home

I went to the lobby and sat in a comfy chair facing the window.

"Hi Honey. How are things going?"

"Hi, Dad. It's going well. My roommate is from Ireland."

"Ireland. Wow, that's exciting. Does she have an accent?"

"Yes, a heavy one. Some people have a hard time understanding her, but I seem to be able to understand her quite well. You know me, I picked up Spanish easily, so maybe it's the same with her accent."

"Perhaps. How's the campus?"

"Nice. I begin classes Monday. I'm going to do a practice run tomorrow by walking from class to class to ensure I know where I am going. Oh, I applied for a job at the library. I'll be notified next week if I get it or not."

"Good choice. You have experience in that area."

I wasn't going to beat around the bush with more small talk.

"Have you decided about the trip yet?"

"I knew there was something I needed to do." He tried to make light of the matter.

"Dad." I scolded. "I'm serious and scared for you. I don't want you to go."

"I know."

"Better safe than sorry."

"I'll let you know."

"When?"

"Soon. Did you get your books?"

I recognized his deliberate change of subject. I believed I had gotten my point across, so I was willing to let it go and move on.

"Yes. I'll give you a call Monday night and let you know how it goes. Love you, Dad."

"I love you too. Bye."

"Bye." I let my phone fall into my lap and heard a familiar voice from above me.

"Checking in with your dad?"

I looked up to see Jasper leaning over the back of the wingback chair looking down at me. He was like a bad penny that seemed to return no matter how many times it was spent, thrown away, or tossed into a well.

"Yes."

He came around the side of my chair, pulled another chair in front of mine, and sat.

"I was just on my way to your room. I wanted to talk with you."

"About what?"

"First, I am sorry for what I said today. Your roommate told me you recently lost your mom. What I said was insensitive and out of line."

"You didn't know, but thanks."

"Do you know what you will be majoring in?"

I took a deep breath trying to release my frustration with my dad's inability to decide and have the patience for small talk with Jasper.

"Since I'm technically a sophomore, I can wait to declare my major at the end of this school year. Have you declared one yet?"

"Business, with a minor in medieval history."

"An interesting combination."

"Yes. I thought business would be practical, but I've always liked history, so I thought I would dual major."

Mom liked history. My, he has the bluest eyes. His scruffy unshaven beard, it's a little rustic, but it looks nice on him too.

Several guys walked through the lobby drawing our attention.

"Hey Jasp, are you coming?"

"Ya, be right there." He turned back to me. "Teammates. We have to go watch the video of today's game."

"Well, I won't keep you." I stood.

"See ya."

"Bye." I watched him jog out the door before returning to my room for a quiet evening.

My Breakfast Companion

My last day to sleep in, well, other than the weekends, and I took full advantage of it. I checked the time on my phone; well past nine o'clock. Mol was still sleeping.

My stomach grumbled.

A bagel with cream cheese and a mocha sounded amazing. It was my go-to breakfast. I dressed quickly and tossed my hair into a bun. *No need for make-up. I'm not trying to impress anyone.*

The cafeteria was nearly empty. Apparently, there weren't too many early risers on a Sunday morning. I grabbed a tray, silverware, and napkins. *They have several flavors of bagels, impressive.* I selected an asiago cheese bagel and inserted it into the toaster. While I waited for it to pop up, I poured myself a mocha from the machine and turned to see Jasper enter the cafeteria. *Be nice, just be friends. And next time, at least put on mascara.*

I watched as he grabbed a tray and went through the breakfast line.

My bagel popped up. I sipped my coffee before placing it on my tray and helping myself to several packets of cream cheese from a bowl. Using the tongs, I removed my bagel, placed it on a plate, and carried my breakfast to a booth.

I spread the cream cheese extra thick onto half of the bagel and took a big bite just as Jasper stood next to me.

"Mind if I join you?"

With my mouth full of food, I motioned toward the empty seat across from me.

"I see you are an early riser like me."

I swallowed what was in my mouth. "Yes, kind of a curse really."

He smiled before cutting into a stack of pancakes and taking a bite.

It looked at the large mound of food on his tray. He had every kind of breakfast food imaginable, except cold cereal.

"I imagine you'll burn off all of those calories during practice."

He looked down to his tray.

"Probably, it's our last two-a-day today. So, you play any sports?"

"I played soccer in high school, but no, I'm focusing on my academics. I plan to jog and work out when I have time."

"If you need someone to work out with, I'll go with you."

"OK."

"What do your classes look like tomorrow?" He shoveled in a forkful of scrambled eggs.

"I have an eight o'clock." I grumbled.

"Eight o'clock classes aren't that bad. A four o'clock class on a Friday is the worst. It gives you such a late start to go home for the weekend. Ideally, having classes only Monday through Thursday is the best schedule, three-day weekends." He grinned.

"I have classes five days a week, but I won't be going home until Christmas break. So, no big deal."

We discovered our home towns were about an hour away from each other. We both disliked lima beans, sushi, and the smell of cigarette smoke. He preferred action movies over my preference romance/drama, yet we both liked comedies. I helped myself to a second mocha while I waited for him to finish eating.

After taking care of our trays, we walked back to the dorm and parted ways. When I reached my door, I looked down the hallway to see Jasper standing at the end. He was staring at me, and he grinned and waved. I returned his wave before opening the door and entering my room.

*   *   *

I smiled confidently as I looked to my spirit guide.

"Well, it looks as if everything is working out as planned."

"*A little too soon to tell. There are choices they must make. We shall wait and see.*"

A Blank Page

I was thankful I'd showered the night before. As expected, I pressed the snooze button twice before forcing myself out of bed. With my clothes already laid out on my desk chair, I headed to the bathroom to dress, returned to get my books, and went to the cafeteria. After my rehearsal yesterday, I had my entire route mapped out with time for lunch and library study time.

There weren't many in the cafeteria. I was thankful. In my haste to be on time to class, I'd failed to put on my makeup. Maybe I could find time in between classes to go back to the dorm and put on my face. I envied people who had dark lashes. My bottom lashes were virtually transparent and always needed a touch of mascara to be seen.

I selected some pancakes, fresh fruit, and orange juice before sitting in an empty booth. I checked my phone before I began to eat. I had twenty minutes.

I watched as others trickled into the cafeteria as if they were sleepwalking. They were struggling with the early start of the day too.

I'll have to grab a mocha in a to-go cup.

My first class was in a building close to the cafeteria. As Mol had predicted, the professor reviewed the syllabus and then assigned a chapter to read and answer the review questions. He didn't keep us for the entire hour, so I went back to my room and applied my makeup before heading to my next class.

The rest of my classes were pretty much the same – syllabus with assigned homework. I went to the library and finished the assigned work before checking my phone for the time and heading toward my last class of the day. Dismissed before 3pm, I could finish my assignments before dinner.

Mol let her fork drop to her plate.

"I'm full."

We relaxed in a cafeteria booth while we discussed the homework from our classes. Our attention was drawn to a noisy group of guys entering the cafeteria. Their hair was wet, and their faces flushed as if they'd had a good work out and just showered. Jasper was with them.

Ah, the soccer team. I sighed and looked toward Mol.

"Are you ready to head back?" I moved my tray to the end of the table and stood. My roommate's face registered disappointment, but she agreed.

Back in our room, I cracked open a textbook and began to read ahead to the next assignment. Mol liked to listen to music while she studied. I preferred it to be quiet. We compromised with her listening through earbuds.

I sent Dad a quick text, 'typical first day of class' before diving into my books.

Laundry Day

Ah, Saturday. I'd made it through the first week of school. Even though it was more work than I'd been responsible for in high school, I was able to keep up with my assignments. I lay awake listening to Mol snore. She'd attended another party last night and woke me when she'd returned to our room. The way she'd stumbled around, I assumed she had been drinking heavily, and God only knows what else.

Not quite ready to get out of bed, I made a mental checklist of what I needed to accomplish over the weekend. Laundry was first on the list. It was still early, so I thought I should try to use the washer and dryer before a line of baskets filled with dirty clothes formed.

My laundry was in my collapsible hamper in the closet. I grabbed a roll of quarters from my underwear drawer, the laundry soap and dryer sheets from the top shelf in the closet and tossed them into the hamper. I looked to my bed and decided not to strip it, knowing it was nearly impossible to do so without waking Mol. I put on my robe and slippers, picked up my hamper, and unlocked the door.

The hallway was as silent as a graveyard. The washer and dryer were idle. I loaded my clothes into the washer, dumped in the soap, inserted the coins, and pushed them into the coin box. The water poured into the tub and I shut the lid. I left my basket with a load of white clothes at the base of the washer before leaving the room.

I was within two steps of my room when I heard the whisper of a familiar voice.

"Hey, you want to get breakfast?"

Jasper was standing at the end of the hall. I groaned, imagining the sight I must be with my hair messed like a rat's nest. My stomach betrayed me as it growled.

I nodded and held up one finger indicated to give me a minute. I searched for a pair of jeans in the closet.

Mol rolled over as I shut my dresser drawer a little too hard while retrieving a sweatshirt.

"What are you doing?"

"Sorry, I'm getting dressed for breakfast. Go back to sleep." I hung up my pajamas and robe on the back of the door, quickly put on mascara with the help of my flashlight on my phone and a mirror Mol had hung on the wall, and ran my fingers through my hair before leaving the room.

Jasper waited in the lobby. He smiled. "I thought I was the only one up this early on a weekend." He opened the door, allowing me to exit first.

While I waited for him to join me, I glanced at my phone for the time estimating my load in the washer would finish in 25 minutes. I needed to return in time to transfer my dark clothes to the dryer and start the second load.

"My incessant internal clock doesn't allow me to sleep in. I thought I would do my laundry before there was a line."

"I have to go to the rink and work this morning."

"Work-study?"

"Yes, I have the same job as I did last year."

"I applied at the library. I'm waiting to hear if I got the job."

I stopped before the cafeteria door and looked to the sidewalk. A feather? I bent down, picked it up, and said a silent thank you as I put it in my pocket. Jasper pulled the handle and reached above my head to hold the door open as I ducked under his arm.

We each took a tray and helped ourselves to what was offered. I eyed the donut with chocolate frosting and sprinkles but thought it would be better to opt for French toast with fruit instead. My morning mocha was becoming an addiction. A good walk around campus in the afternoon should help offset the calories. I took an extra banana for a mid-afternoon snack before carrying my tray to the nearest booth.

I couldn't help but notice Jasper's heaping tray of food as he placed it upon the table. *I could never eat all of that.* He noticed me staring at it as he sat opposite me.

"Remember, breakfast is the most important meal of the day." He winked as he picked up his fork from the tray and smiled, displaying perfect white teeth and a dimple in his cheek.

I was certain my face flushed a rosy pink.

Our conversation was light, and he did most of the talking. He told me about his family and his home town. I did the same, but I avoided any details about Mom. At times, it still hurt to talk about her.

We talked about our classes, activities on campus, clubs to join, and sporting events. He lowered his voice as a few girls walked by our booth.

"Hi, Jasper." They waved and smiled.

Jasper nodded his head as he continued talking.

A blonde, carrying her tray, stopped at our table interrupting our conversation.

"Good luck at your game this afternoon."

"Thanks." He stared at me as if he didn't want to make eye contact with the pretty blonde.

I had finished eating and checked the time on my phone.

"If you'll excuse me, my laundry is done, and I don't want to keep anyone waiting. They may end up tossing my clean clothes on the folding table or the floor." I moved my tray to the end of the table and stood. Jasper had yet to finish eating.

The dim-witted blonde slid into my vacated seat.

"Oh, are you leaving?"

Yes, Miss Obvious, I'm leaving. I looked toward Jasper's pleading face. He wasn't pleased. I could tell he didn't want to talk to his new breakfast partner. A pang of guilt almost made me feel sorry for him. I lifted my tray from the table.

"Sorry, have fun at work." I took care of my tray and left.

After putting my clothes in the dryer and starting my next load, I returned to my room to find my roommate gone. *Probably in the bathroom.*

My phone rang. It was Dad.

"Hello, Dad."

"Hello. Did I wake you?"

"No. I got up early to do my laundry."

"I thought I would call you and tell you I won't be going to Las Vegas."

I let out a sigh of relief. "Good, but you still need to write a will and make a record of the bills that need to be paid and when. It's important."

"I know. It's something I've putting off for a long time."

"Promise me you will get it done soon."

"I promise."

There was a knock at my door.

"I got to go. I love you, Dad."

"I love you too."

I opened the door as I ended my call and looked up at Jasper's sarcastic smile. He seemed a little out of breath, as if he had run back from the cafeteria.

"Thanks a lot." He leaned his shoulder on the doorframe.

I chuckled. "What? You didn't want to spend some quality time with a gorgeous blonde who thinks the sun rises and sets in your stunning baby blue eyes?"

He raised one eyebrow and frowned.

I took a step backward to allow him to enter. "Would you like to come in?" My tone was sarcastic.

"No, I have to get to work."

"I'm sorry, but I really had to put my wash in the dryer. There were two other laundry baskets in line for the washer and I still had another load to do." I snickered. "I take it you aren't very fond of her?"

"She's a stalker."

"Sorry."

"No big deal. She's my problem, not yours."

Mol entered. Clearly, she had a hangover as she pushed, insistently squeezed, between Jasper and the doorframe, holding her head and groaning.

"Hi, Jasper."

"Hi, Mol." He looked back at me. "Well, I have to get to the rink. See you two later?"

Mol fell into bed.

"Later."

A Change Of Season

The following weeks seemed to fly by as my schedule became busier with juggling classes, homework, and working in the library. I monitored the news, but nothing occurred in Las Vegas the weekend Dad's family was there. My theory was, the reason nothing bad happened was because the fourth ticket was not purchased. Either the lone wolf was caught, or whatever he was up to was called off.

The trees were changing color, days growing shorter, and there was a crispness in the morning air. Mom loved autumn. It was her favorite season. Her birthday was coming up soon, the second after her death.

FROM BEYOND THE GRAVE

It was Saturday, laundry day. I got out of bed early, dressed, and applied mascara. With Mom in mind, I looked to my desk where my whiteboard rested against the wall. The plastic sandwich bag of feathers I had collected over the past month was attached to it with a magnet. I knew it seemed silly to keep every feather I found, but each one seemed special.

I started my laundry and met Jasper in the lobby. Eating breakfast together had become a welcomed habit. However, the girls who constantly hounded him were annoying. He and I were friends, nothing more, but our friendship was growing stronger. I hoped to attend his home soccer games during the remainder of the season and planned to ask for those hours off from my job in the library.

After taking a drink, Jasper set his glass of orange juice on his tray.

"I'll be leaving on Friday for the weekend. I won't be back until Sunday afternoon. An away game," he explained between a bite of scrambled eggs.

"OK, Good luck."

"Thanks."

I looked at the booth across from us. His dimwitted fan club was staring, whispering, and laughing. "I assume they won't be following you to your game."

He glanced in the direction of my reference.

"Thank God."

*   *   *

I was working in the library on Friday morning shelving a book when I looked to the floor and found a feather.

"Thank you." I whispered as I put it in my back jean pocket, pushed the cart to the next aisle, and shelved another book. I felt a tap on my shoulder and turned to see Jasper.

"Hey, what's up?" I laid the book on the cart.

"I wanted to say goodbye before getting on the bus."

We had exchanged phone numbers a few weeks ago. He could have sent a text.

"Have a safe trip and good luck." I grabbed the book from the cart and read the filing code on the spine.

"Thanks. I'll see you on Sunday."

"OK, bye."

"Bye." He paused as if he wanted to say something more but turned and left. One of his ogling fans stepped into the opening of the aisle, watched as Jasper left, and looked toward me, glaring resentfully. Ignoring her, I redirected my attention to filing the book in my hand to its proper location.

*   *   *

We hovered at the opposite end of the aisle.

"Oh, this is frustrating. How can she not see that he likes her?"

"*He has chosen, but she has yet to do so.*"

"That's obvious."

"*He must make his intentions known, remove her blindfold, and open her heart.*"

*   *   *

It was strange eating breakfast by myself on Saturday. I continued to receive glaring stares from Jasper's fan club and did my best to ignore them. My attention was drawn to a tall guy entering the cafeteria. He was cute, very cute.

I had dallied long enough. I checked my phone, ate quickly, and left to finish my laundry before I had to report for work in the library.

My Romantic Misconception

Mol and I were eating dinner when the guy I'd seen at breakfast entering the cafeteria, which caused me to stop talking in midsentence.

Mol looked over her shoulder to see what had drawn my attention. She turned back toward me.

"Oh, my, he is cute. Shall I introduce you?"

"Do you know him?"

"It doesn't matter. Stay put. I'll be right back."

"Mol…" I could feel the heat rising in my face, certain it was turning red, as I watched her approach the guy and lead him to our table. Mol motioned toward me.

"I'd like you to meet Elizabeth. Elizabeth, I'd like you to meet, um, what was your name again?"

It was obvious Mol didn't know the guy. It was obvious to him as well. He extended his hand and took mine within his.

"Hi, I'm Tom."

"Hi."

Mol extended her hand toward him.

"Well, hello Tom, I'm Mol. Would you like to join us for dinner?"

He looked at both of us and our trays of food, half eaten.

"Sure, be right back." He left to get in line.

I glared at Mol, keeping the aggravation within my voice at a whisper. "What are you doing?"

She grinned displaying a sarcastic innocent look upon her face. "I thought you wanted to meet him."

"I just think he's cute. I don't necessarily want to meet him. I'm not that forward."

Mol picked up her fork and waved it toward me. "I just took the first step for you. It's up to you to make something of it." She started shoveling food into her mouth. By the time Tom got to our table, she was nearly finished eating. She grabbed the pear from her tray, placed it in her jacket pocket, and stood as he approached our table. My eyes enlarged. *How dare she leave me alone with him*?

"Here, Tom, you can take my seat. I'm finished."

Tom looked to Mol, to me, then back to Mol.

"Are you sure? You don't have to run off on my account."

"No, it's fine. I have to get back anyway." Mol winked at me.

I scowled as Tom sat down in the vacated seat and looked toward me.

"She set us up, didn't she?"

"Yes, sorry about that."

"That's fine. I was going to eat alone anyway. I'm glad for the company."

*   *   *

"Another lesson?" I looked at my spirit guide.

"*Yes.*"

"Something tells me this experience is going to be an unpleasant, emotional one."

"*Perhaps. She must learn the difference between a crush, true love, and what she is willing to tolerate in a relationship.*"

"Something I recall learning as well."

*   *   *

I stared at his chiseled chin moving up and down with each bite of food he ate. His shoulders were broad and muscular. Like most of the students attending the university, I assumed he was an athlete, but which sport?

"I play baseball." He read my mind.

"I assumed you played some type of sport."

"Yes, I just got done working out. I have to keep in shape during the offseason."

"I played soccer in high school."

"Oh, you're just a freshman. I'm a junior."

"What are you majoring in?"

"Sports medicine, but I plan on coaching someday."

"Kind of a risky career, isn't it? I mean, how will you find a job once you graduate?"

"Oh, I'll get a job. Maybe even coach here someday. The coach likes me. He'll hire me for sure."

I finished eating and waited politely while he ate. He threw his fork onto his plate.

"Well, I'm full. I'll walk you back to your dorm."

After taking care of our trays, it was a short walk before we stood in front of my dorm.

"So, this is your place."

"Yes."

"I'll call you for a date some time."

"Sure." We exchanged numbers before I opened the door and entered.

Mol looked up from the textbook she was reading.

"Well? How did it go?"

"He's nice and very cute." I sighed.

"Oh, goodness. You're in love."

"I just met the guy. How can you tell if I'm in love?"

"You have that look in your eyes."

My cellphone rang. The caller ID indicated it was Tom. I looked at Mol.

"It's him." My stomach fluttered, almost somersaulted. I couldn't keep the smile off my face as I answered. "Hello."

"I had a date cancel on me. How about we go out tonight, or better yet, you come by my place."

I looked at the window. It was beginning to rain. *A little rain never hurt anyone. I'm not made of sugar.*

"OK. What time?" I grinned at Mol.

"Let's say 8?"

"OK 8. See you then."

"I'll text you my address." He hung up before I could reply. I check the time. It was 7:30. I touched up my make-up, changed my shirt, and put on my raincoat with its protective hood before heading out into the rainy night. I had to stop by a 'you are here' sign to find his dorm, then negotiate the hallways until I found his room. Taking a deep breath, I knocked. He opened it.

"You're a little late." He motioned for me to enter. "Let me take your coat."

I slipped it off and handed it to him.

"I thought we were going out."

"Naw, I don't have any money for that. We can just chill here."

His reasoning was understandable. Most college students didn't have much money to spend. But then again, why did he ask me out?

He turned on the TV with the remote and plopped down on the coach. Uncertain of what to do, I scanned the room before looking at him. He patted the seat next to him, indicating where I should sit.

I did as he requested. His arm dropped down on my shoulders pulling me next to him. It felt good to be close, secure, and he smelled amazing too. Before long he lifted my chin with his hand and began kissing me. I was lowered down to my back as he continued to probe my mouth with his tongue. His hands were demanding as they fondled my breasts and began lifting my shirt. Panic rose within me. This wasn't what I'd expected. It made me feel uncomfortable, used, and sleazy. I pushed him away from me and rolled out from beneath him, falling to the floor. I was shaking inside as I stood.

"I thought this was going to be a date, not molestation." I grabbed my coat from the hook where it hung.

"I'm sorry, princess, but you were the one who came to me. I didn't expect you'd be a big tease."

"And I didn't expect you to be an egotistical asshole. Don't worry. It won't happen again." I left the room slamming the door behind me. My hands were shaking. Tears brimmed in my eyes. My heart raced as I hurried toward my dorm. My hood fell off my head. I could barely see where I was going as the rain continued to fall. My vision was clouded by my welling tears that spilled onto my cheeks.

I bumped into someone. A hand grabbed my arm and spun me around, and I swung my arm ready to throw a punch as I tried to pull away.

"Woah, Elizabeth, it's me."

Jasper's voice registered within my mind. I wiped my eyes and kept my face downward. I didn't want him to see the emotional upheaval I was experiencing.

"Are you OK?" Once he realized I had regained my sense of balance, he released my arm.

"Yes." I lied. The shakiness in my voice betrayed me as well.

"You're not OK. What's wrong?"

"I don't want to talk about it."

"Well, if that's…"

"Guys are assholes!"

He scowled. "I'll try not to take that personally."

"Sorry, not you."

"My dad says, 'there's an asshole in every crowd', and I guess you found one tonight. I assume it was a date that went wrong?"

"Yes, Mol set me up."

"Personally, I question her taste in men. She seems like the outgoing type, but one who may sleep around with anyone."

"She isn't picky." I looked at my surroundings, then to him, puzzled. "I thought you weren't going to be back until tomorrow."

"The bus got back tonight. I was just on my way to the dorm. Shall we walk together to ensure you there safe and sound on this dreary night?"

Gallant as always. I grinned. His concern for me was genuine and appreciated. I guess I hadn't thought about Tom possibly following me, seeking what he thought I should have given him.

"Sure. Thanks."

We walked in silence. Jasper glanced toward me from the corner of his eye.

"Do you want to talk about it?"

"Not really."

We continued toward the dorm. Maybe I was in shock as I began muttering to myself. "I was just stupid."

"Who was the guy?"

"Someone I saw in the cafeteria. All I said was that I thought he was cute. Mol took it upon herself to introduce me. It was supposed to be a date, a date, but he wanted, well, you know. I'm not that type."

"Gotcha."

"I was just so stupid."

"You're not stupid. It was unexpected, and you didn't really know the guy." He paused and glanced toward me, hesitant to state his next question. "I assume nothing happened?"

"Nothing happened, fortunately. My virtue is still intact." *I can't believe I just admitted to him my virginal status.*

"Good, so is mine."

He's a virgin too? He must be kidding.

Jasper jumped over a puddle on the sidewalk. "You have a kind heart. Maybe you just see the good in everyone, but not everyone is good."

"Yes, I learned that the hard way."

"At least you learned." He chuckled.

A chuckle escaped me. I smiled. I was thankful Jasper could make light of the situation I had gotten myself into and overlook my stupidity and lack of experience in reading someone.

He held open the door for me to pass through into the lobby.

I turned to wait for him and noticed he was wearing a suit. "You look nice."

Surprise registered on his face. "Thanks." His grin seemed forced, yet polite as he looked toward my face. "The rain has melted your mascara. Perhaps you would like to stop at the restroom and wash your face."

I went into the bathroom, looked at my face in the mirror, and groaned. My mascara had made black streaks down my cheeks. I took a rough, brown paper towel and soap and washed until my cheeks were pink. I exited to find him still standing outside the door.

"Any better?"

He put his index finger under my chin, turned my face right, then left. "Much, now I can see your beautiful face." He motioned toward my room.

"I'm not beautiful." I dismissed the compliment. I never thought of myself as beautiful.

He stopped walking and held his arms wide. "What? You think I'm lying?"

I turned around and walked backward. "Just a bit. I'm not beautiful."

His mouth fell agape. "Well, apparently you haven't seriously looked in the mirror lately, Miss Elizabeth, because you are beautiful."

I scowled, turned around, and continued walking.

Within a stride or two, he caught up with me. "You really don't believe me?"

"No."

"Well, let me ask you this. Do you think I'm cute? Maybe even handsome?"

I laughed as I looked at him uncertain of what he was trying to get me to admit. I hesitated.

161

He waited with a silly smirk on his face. "Come on. Be honest. I can take it."

"Fine. I think you are very cute and attractively handsome. The combination of your dark curly hair and baby blue eyes is mesmerizing, quite stunning. Girls must be falling all over themselves for a moment of your time, yearn for you to look their way, and eager to warm your bed." *Good lord, I sounded like I was quoting one of Mom's historical romance novels.*

"In truth, no one has ever described me as you just did. And that's the second time you have mentioned the color of my eyes. For your information, I don't have women standing in line for a moment of my attention. There are a few who would like my attention, but I have little interest in giving them any."

"Oh, your stalkers." I chuckled.

"Yes, my stalkers. In truth, I would never date a woman who easily goes to bed with guys. They can't be trusted in a relationship."

"Interesting perspective, I must agree."

"Do you know what I find most beautiful about you, other than your face?"

Oh God, here it comes. "I would be surprised if you found anything, but let's hear it." I inserted my key into the door and looked at him.

"Miss Elizabeth, I find you to be the most beautiful woman I have ever met. The golden, sun-bleached streaks in your hair glisten in the moonlight and your blue-violet orbs appear as deep as the ocean. Your heart is pure. You are kind and thoughtful and focused on what you want to achieve in life. All admirable qualities. And your best feature, I believe, is your bottom. It's quite cute." He winked at the conclusion of his dramatic confession.

I turned the key in the door and pushed it open. Mol, I assumed, was out for the evening. She had left a lamp on.

"My butt?" I laughed as I stepped into the room.

"Yes, I'm a butt man and you have a rather nice one." He stood in the doorway. I turned to see his head tilted to the side with his pinky finger poised at the corner of his mouth. He was staring at my behind.

"Very funny." I hung up my wet coat.

His arms and fingers spread wide as he pleaded his innocence stepping into the room.

"I'm being totally serious." He had conveyed his true feelings but thought to keep the mood light by changing the subject. "Well, shall we watch some TV? Maybe there's a good movie on or something." He took off his suit coat and placed it over the back of my desk chair.

"Sure. We can make some popcorn."

I handed him the remote while I placed a bag of popcorn in the microwave.

He began flipping through the channels. "What do you like to watch?"

"I'm not too picky but prefer not to watch anything violent. People getting killed and tortured isn't my favorite form of entertainment."

"Mine either. I don't mind suspenseful and spooky though." He scanned the guide and selected the channel. "How about this?"

I watched the screen a few moments before retrieving a large plastic bowl from the top of the closet.

"Perfect. I haven't seen it before." The microwave dinged. I dumped the contents of the bag into the bowl and placed it next to him on the futon that Mol and I had recently purchased. "Oh, you want something to drink?" I crossed the room.

"Water if you have it, please."

I grabbed two bottles of water from the refrigerator and handed him one. He placed the bowl of popcorn in his lap so that I could sit next to him.

We finished watching the movie and the one that followed too. As the second movie neared its end, my eyes began to involuntarily close. I tried to camouflage several yawns. As the movie ended, Jasper rose.

"Well, sleepyhead, I hate to leave you alone, but it's getting late and I have to report to work early in the morning. Knowing Mol, she will be out partying until the wee hours of the morning so lock the door when I leave."

"If she makes it home." I grinned. "Thanks for walking me home. It was a knightly gesture on my behalf, kind sir."

"My pleasure, my lady." He bowed.

I smiled. "Good night, Jasper."

He retrieved his suit coat from the chair. "Good night, Elizabeth."

I walked him to the door and closed it behind him. I hoped Mol wasn't too intoxicated to use her key to get into the room, and I turned the lock until I heard it click.

Becoming A Fan

The week was a busy one with classes, tests, work, studying, and more tests.

On Saturday, Mom's birthday, I woke and went to my computer. I posted on my social media page a heartfelt birthday wish hoping my love for her could reach all the way to heaven.

Happy Birthday to my mom in heaven! I hope you're enjoying your favorite glass of wine as you watch over us from above. Please try not to laugh as we stumble our way through life. I love you and miss you.

I wiped a tear away from my eye before getting dressed, starting my laundry, and meeting Jasper for breakfast in the lobby. He greeted me with his usual upbeat self.

"Good morning, Elizabeth."

"Morning." I wasn't in the mood to talk as we walked to the cafeteria and entered. As was his habit, he held the door open for me to pass before him.

"Are you OK? You seem a little down." He knew me better then I knew myself.

"I'm fine. Just remembering my mom. It would have been her birthday today."

He remained quiet as he took two trays from the stack, handed one to me, and we got in line. "Well, happy birthday to your mom."

When I looked up at him, he smiled kindly.

After getting our food and sitting down, the dimwitted brunette walked by our table and batted her eyelashes.

"Hi, Jasper."

He didn't reply, just nodded.

I watched as she sat in the booth across from where we were sitting. She strategically placed herself in the seat where she could ogle at Jasper, ensuring he could see her as well.

I stared in disbelief. *How can she be so forward? She just doesn't get it. He wants nothing to do with her.* My face must have conveyed what I was thinking.

"Hey, just ignore her." Jasper scooped a forkful of scrambled eggs.

"She's pretty persistent. Don't you get tired of it? I mean, it's like she is stalking you."

He swallowed his mouthful of food. "Do you want me to talk to her?"

I sighed and looked to the ceiling and then down to my plate. "No, that may only encourage her."

He reached into his pants back pocket and laid two tickets before me on the table.

"I managed to snag these for you and Mol for the soccer game this afternoon. I hope you don't have to work."

"I do, but not until tonight."

"I have to be there before the game to warm-up, but I'll meet you afterward outside of the locker room."

"OK." I slid the tickets toward me and read the time of the game. "Thanks. I'm looking forward to watching you play."

*   *   *

Mol and I found a seat in the bleachers.

I could hardly believe my eyes as the brunette and her groupies sat on the seat in front of us. After the singing of the national anthem and the game began, they cheered for Jasper every time he got the ball.

Mol leaned toward me. "Do you want to move?"

"No, they will probably just move with us. It's obvious she wants me to know she has a thing for Jasper, like it wasn't apparent before."

"She must think of you as a threat."

"A threat?"

"Yeah, you know, like Jasper is in love with you and not her. Like you are stealing him away from her."

"Then she needs to wise up. She never had him. And he's not in love with me anyway. We're just friends."

Mol looked toward me, tilted her head, and displayed an all-knowing smile, which I disregarded.

Despite the noisy fan club sitting in front of me, I focused on the game and Jasper's play. He was good, very good, and an aggressive, talented player. He had several breakaways. I stood and cheered as I watched him charge down the field, pass the ball, receive it back, and score a goal, which was the game-winner.

Mol and I waited for Jasper after the game. It took a long time for the players to emerge from their locker room. I was certain they were showering, at least I hoped so. I could see the brunette and her minions huddled to one side of the locker room door, ready to pounce once Jasper appeared. They would occasionally look in my direction and then talk amongst themselves.

Mol noticed their chattering too. "Bitches be jealous." She chuckled.

Waiting for Jasper under the watchful eyes and gossiping mouths of the groupies was intimidating. I was thankful Mol was with me, otherwise I would have walked back to the dorm without waiting. Eventually, the players began to trickle out of the locker room, their faces flushed and hair damp. Dressed in their suits, they were greeted by their parents and friends and congratulated on a game well played. I saw Jasper as he stepped through the doorway. His dark, curly hair glistened in the afternoon sun. Searching the crowd, he nodded as he spied us and headed in our direction. The brunette and her groupies pushed their way forward and stepped in front of him, blocking his way.

I had to give him credit. He took a moment to politely thank them for attending, dismissed them quickly, and wove through the people toward me and Mol. I had to admit, he looked like a magazine cover model in his suit with his loosely curled damp dark hair and striking blue eyes.

"Good game, Jasper." Mol kiddingly punched him on his arm. "I'm going to head back to the room."

Jasper looked to Mol. "Thanks, and thanks for coming to the game."

Suspicious of the motive for her sudden departure, I glanced at my roommate as she winked and walked away.

"See ya, Mol." I turned to Jasper. "Good game. Nice goal."

"Thanks."

I looked past him to see his groupies give me the evil eye. "Your number one fan sat right in front of me during the entire game. I think she has a crush on you." I laughed as we began walking to the dorm.

He stopped walking. "You know, that's the first time I have heard you laugh. You have a great laugh." He jogged the few steps to join me.

"I'm glad you like it."

"I do, and I hope to hear more of it in the future."

Heard From Above

I was usually a sound sleeper, but early Tuesday morning I woke during the night and checked my cell phone for the time. It was 3am. One thought resonated within my mind.

'*You're doing fine and I'm proud of you.*'

Mom. The message was from her. In fact, I was certain of it. I could only surmise the justification for her message was in response to my post, my heartfelt post. Would she continue to watch over me and respond to others I sent to her? A calmness settled within me, enabling me to drift back to sleep.

*   *   *

I descended from her dorm room ceiling.

"I'm glad she understood my message and that it was from me."

"*You have always been divinely connected.*"

"I meant what I said. I'm very proud of her."

"*As you should be. May your pride continue to give her strength and comfort throughout her life.*"

I looked to my spirit guide, puzzled by the reason she would need additional strength and comfort. Did he know something that I did not?

*   *   *

I attended nearly all of Jasper's remaining home soccer games. His gaggle of groupies continued their persistent pursuit both at breakfast and at his games.

As we walked back to the dorm after his last game of the season, he was acting oddly, unusually quiet, and maybe a little nervous. Mol had a cold, so she'd opted out of attending. She lay in bed with a box of facial tissue nearby. I shivered as a gust of crisp autumn wind blew my hair into my eyes. Brushing it aside, I looked to Jasper.

"You played a good game, as always."

"Thanks. I'm glad you were there watching. It means a lot to me."

"Well, you know, I didn't have anything else to do this afternoon, so why not. It just so happened that this superstar soccer player gave me a free ticket to attend." I glanced toward him to see a silly smirk on his face. Was he blushing? "Besides, the more I'm around Mol, the more likely I'm going to catch whatever she has."

When we stepped inside the lobby, I stopped at the entrance to my hallway.

"I'd invite you to my room, but Mol, well, you don't want to get sick too."

"Do you want to hang out in my room?"

It was the first time he had invited me to his room. I'd never thought to ask if he had a roommate. My curiosity was piqued. Was he a slob with dirty clothes strewn about the floor, or was his room orderly and clean?

"OK, but let me check on Mol. I'll be right back." He waited at the end of the hall while I went into our room to find Mol sleeping. I decided not to wake her. I would text her later. I locked the door as I left and joined Jasper in the lobby.

"How is she?"

"Sleeping, so I didn't wake her. I can check in on her later."

We walked down a hallway and turned the corner into the next. His room was near the end. He unlocked the door, pushed it open, and allowed me to enter first.

The floor was void of dirty clothes, bed made, and books filed neatly on the shelf above his desk. The other desk contained a microwave. On its shelf were various food products. I looked at the top bunk. The mattress was bare. I heard the closet door slide open and turned to see him hang up his suit coat.

"You have a private room?"

"I had a roommate at the beginning of the semester, but he decided college wasn't for him and went home." He held out his hand to accept my coat, which I slid from my shoulders and gave it to him.

"Thanks."

"Sure." He hung it in his closet and turned to see me standing. "Have a seat." He motioned toward a contemporary loveseat against the wall. "You want something to drink?"

"Water, if you have it." I sat while he retrieved two bottles of water from the mini refrigerator.

"There's something I've been wanting to ask you." He twisted the cap to open the bottle before handing it to me and sitting at the other end of the small couch.

I sensed a seriousness in his voice.

"OK."

"Most of the guys are bringing a date to the soccer banquet. I was wondering if you would like to be my plus one? I'll understand if you say no. These things can be kind of boring."

I had to agree with him. Soccer banquets were a little boring, but after attending several of my own, at least I knew what to expect.

"Sure, I'd be happy to go with you."

"Great. Oh, and my parents will be there as well."

Huh, didn't expect that. I took a calming breath. "Nice, I'll get to meet them."

*   *   *

As I readied for the banquet the following Saturday afternoon, my palms were sweaty. I suspected I may have applied my deodorant several times too. I held each dress in my closet before me as I looked in the mirror. I couldn't decide which one to wear. One made me look like a nun, another a hooker. After laying out my top three choices on the futon, Mol contributed her choice and I immediately put it back in the closet. In the end, I chose the cranberry color dress because it went best with my complexion. I styled my hair and ensured my make-up wasn't overdone or washed out, before putting on a nice yet subdued shade of lipstick.

I was startled by the knock at the door. Mol opened it and Jasper walked in. His mouth fell open.

"Wow, you look amazing."

I smiled. His opinion was a bit biased. Nevertheless, it was nice to hear and helped to boost my confidence.

"Thank you." I grabbed my coat from the closet and cursed internally, wishing I had brought my dress coat from home. I slipped my arm into the sleeve as Jasper held up the remainder of my coat, helping me put it on. He bent his right arm.

"My lady, shall we be off?" Displaying a silly grin, he put me at ease.

I laced my arm within his. "Sure."

Mol grabbed her phone. "Wait, let me get a picture of your first official date."

I cringed internally as we posed, and she captured the moment.

"Bye, you two. Have fun!"

Fun? At sports banquet? I gave my roommate a hesitant crooked smile. "Thanks, Mol."

A black four-door BMW was waiting outside of our dorm. Jasper opened the back door, allowing me to seat myself. The man behind the wheel remained silent and looked straight ahead. The woman in the passenger seat glanced over her shoulder as Jasper entered the other side of the car, joining me.

"Mom, Dad, this is Elizabeth." He turned to me. "My Mom and Dad."

His dad just nodded his head. His mother turned in her seat to get a better look at me.

"It's nice to meet you, Elizabeth."

"It's nice to meet you both."

With niceties out of the way, his father drove us to the banquet. Tension masking my face, Jasper reached across the seat, clasped my hand, and winked. I tried to smile but didn't think I pulled it off well. I tried to calm myself, but then it dawned on me. Jasper may have to sit with his team, and I would be left to entertain his parents. Much to my relief, each player was assigned to sit with their parents and or guests.

The meal was nice but eating it was a challenge. Was I being cross-examined in a courtroom? His dad fired questions in succession without looking up from his plate while he continued to eat. Unable to take a bite of food, I put my fork down as I divulged my education, possible undergraduate major, my consideration to pursue a master's degree, and my family. Jasper tried to stop the line of questioning, but his father just spoke over him. Mr. McLean was a little stunned, and even stopped chewing his steak and looked up at me, when I informed him of my mother's recent death. I tried to check the defensiveness in my voice, challenging him for his rude intrusiveness into my personal loss. His questions stopped. I was able to resume eating, but unfortunately, my food was cold.

Once our plates were cleared and dessert served, the award portion of the banquet began. Jasper was called to the podium several times to receive an award.

His parents drove us back to the dorm, dropped us off, and headed home. As I watched their car leave, Jasper waved before turning toward me.

"So, what did you think of my parents?" We walked into the lobby.

I sighed, finally being able to relax. I glanced up at him as I took a deep breath before giving my full assessment.

"They seem nice. I felt like I was walking on eggshells. I mean, your mom scrutinized every word I said, every movement I made as if she was assessing my net worth or waiting for me to do something stupid. And your dad, I think he didn't like me at all. He barely made eye contact, like he didn't want to be bothered with me other than to pry into my personal life as if he was evaluating my breeding."

"Mom's just being protective of her little baby boy."

"Like I'm some type of venomous viper? Goodness, we're just friends." I turned toward my room.

Jasper glanced toward me with a sly flirtatious grin before he continued. "And Dad, well, he's just being Dad. All business. Anyway, it doesn't matter what they think." He smiled as he shrugged his shoulder and tilted his head close enough to my ear that I could feel his warm breath upon my cheek. "Thanks for being my date."

Staring into his baby blue eyes, I smiled. *Date?*

"You're welcome."

*   *   *

Now that soccer was over, Jasper spent more time with Mol and me. He would occasionally stop in the library and visit while I worked. I discovered more about his true character every day. He was sensitive, driven, and thoughtful. I found his sense of humor most amusing and at times appreciated. Our dinners together were enjoyable, and he often had me laughing through tears.

With Thanksgiving break next week, I didn't want Mol to be alone for the long weekend.

"Do you have any plans during break? I know you mentioned traveling, but we are only off for five days."

"I thought about going to New York and seeing Rockefeller Center, but I can do that over Christmas break when I'll have more time. So, no plans, really, other than staying here."

"Good, then why don't you come home with me? You can celebrate Thanksgiving with my family."

With classes concluded until after break, we loaded up the car and I drove home. I never thought much of our house. It was old with a lot of detailed woodwork, but Mol thought it was impressive.

"Your house is so nice. Much bigger than my apartment at home."

Spooky greeted me as I set my laundry and duffle bag on the kitchen floor and I picked him up. He was thin, thinner than he'd been before I left for college. *Poor old kitty.* I could feel his ribs, which made me question if he had been eating properly, or if my brother hadn't taken the time to feed him his usual treats.

After giving Mol a tour of the house and putting our dirty laundry in the laundry room, I called Dad at work.

"I'm home."

"Good. Is your roommate with you?"

"Yes."

"Well, Grandma has invited us over for Thanksgiving tomorrow. Give her a call and let her know we have one more for dinner. You may want to offer to make a dish to pass too."

"OK." I looked at Mol. "We're having dinner tomorrow at my grandma's house. I have to let her know you are coming too." I dialed her landline and waited as her phone rang several times.

"Well, hello you."

"Hi. My roommate came home with me for the weekend, so we have one more for dinner."

"Oh, how nice. I look forward to meeting her."

"What dish would you like us to bring?" I opened the refrigerator to see what was inside. As expected, it was nearly empty except for beer, candy bars, a pizza box, and condiments.

"Oh, I don't know. How about you make the mashed potatoes and gravy, sweet potato casserole, and a couple of pumpkin pies?"

My mouth fell open. *All of that?* I went to the pantry, which was nearly empty as well.

"OK."

"Great. Thank you. See you tomorrow at 4."

"Bye."

"Bye-bye."

I set my phone on the kitchen counter and looked to Mol.

"Looks as if we will be spending most of today grocery shopping and cooking food for tomorrow." I took Mom's recipe box from the cupboard, pulled the recipes, and made of list of ingredients we needed. After a quick trip to the grocery store, we made two pumpkin and one apple pie and prepared the potatoes and sweet potatoes for baking tomorrow. We also made a nice dinner for all of us to enjoy.

*   *   *

We inhaled the aroma of roasted turkey as we entered Grandma's house, each carrying a dish or two to pass. Her dining room table was covered with a festive tablecloth of autumn colors. There were placemats, folded cloth napkins, and stacked plates at each place setting on the table. In the center was a beautiful bouquet of orange, red, and yellow flowers. She liked to go all out when she entertained.

Even though Mol spoke English, Grandma had difficulty deciphering her heavy Irish accent. I tried not to laugh as

Grandma would look to me to interpret Mol's reply to her prying questions.

Dinner was placed on the table, and we sat, and watched Dad carve the turkey. There wasn't much carving involved. The meat fell off the bones. Grandma had made homemade rolls, my favorite, smothered with real butter. We served the typical Thanksgiving menu, but to Mol, it was a real treat.

I tried not to overeat, but the food was delicious, much more flavorful than the cafeteria food. There was always the conundrum I seemed to encounter, in having just enough cranberry sauce for the last bite of turkey or just enough turkey for the last bite of cranberry sauce. I finally stopped eating when my stomach began to ache. Mol and I helped Grandma clear the table, put away leftovers, and wash the dishes.

With our bellies full, we waited to have the pies with freshly made whipped cream. Dad laid on the couch and took a nap while the rest of us played a game of Aggravation.

After my brother won the game, we put it away while Grandma sliced the pies. My cell phone rang. I looked to the caller ID to see Jasper was calling. I went to one of Grandma's bedrooms to talk to him privately.

"Hi, Jasper."

"Hi. Happy Thanksgiving."

"Same to you."

"So, did you eat yet?"

"Yes, we ate our meal earlier. We are going to have our dessert in a minute. You?"

"We're just sitting down to eat."

"I see. I assume the traditional turkey dinner?"

"Pretty much. Oh, they are calling me for dinner. I'll see you on Sunday."

"OK, bye."

"Bye."

When I returned to the dining room, Grandma was placing my dessert on the table and looked toward me.

"So, when are we going to meet Jasper?"

I groaned internally as I looked to Mol, who gave me an apologetic, guilty grimace. Apparently, Grandma had pressured her into revealing who had called me. I looked back to Grandma.

"I'm not quite sure. He is spending the holiday with his family. He's just a friend."

Mol looked down at her dessert, hoping the smile upon her face wouldn't be noticed. She quickly took a large bite of pumpkin pie topped with whipped cream to avoid being cross-examined by Grandma.

*   *   *

"I miss being with them, celebrating with them." I hovered over to the opposite side of the room.

"*You are there. Albeit, they cannot see you.*"

I looked at my husband. There was something different about him, but I couldn't determine the cause. Was he unwell? I looked to his spirit guide hovering near the ceiling, who nodded his head in confirmation. I looked back to my spirit guide.

"*His time is drawing near.*"

"So soon? But the children are still young. They need him."

"*It is as they have chosen. His departure from this life was determined before his birth and will occur once his purpose is fulfilled. Your children knew this before they chose the two of you as parents.*"

I wanted to spare them the heartache, the grief, of losing another parent.

"Is there anything that can be done to intervene, maybe prolong his life?"

My spirit guide looked toward my husband's spirit guide. Both nodded their heads before a vision appeared.

*   *   *

Grandma filled a paper bag with containers of leftovers for us to take home. Our family celebrations always involved too much food for us to eat and she was unable to eat what was left over all by herself. I was certain the containers would be empty within a day or two, especially the pies. Once home, the leftovers were put in the refrigerator. I couldn't stop myself from grabbing one of Grandma's rolls and smothering it with butter for a snack while we watched TV.

I lay in bed that night listening to Mol snoring on the blow-up mattress on the floor next to my bed. Maybe her consumption of turkey had helped her fall to sleep quickly. Thanksgiving. What was I thankful for? My father, brother, and Grandmother, Spooky, the time I had with my mother and the memories, my job and the opportunity to go to college, and... Jasper. The thought of him made me smile. I stared at the back of my eyelids trying to fall asleep. Was it my imagination, or did I see white streaks of light toward a focal point and feel as if I was falling, until I was surrounded by darkness?

~

"Mom?" She stood before me, holding a large container of vitamin C tablets.

"Have your father begin taking these." She handed them to me.

I looked down at the plastic container before looking to her face.

"Is he sick?"

"Insist that he take them." She faded into the darkness.

~

Mol was still sleeping when I joined Dad for breakfast.

"I saw Mom last night." I placed a piece of pumpkin pie on a plate and topped it with whipped cream; breakfast of champions.

"Really? What did she say?" He put two slices of bread in the toaster and pushed the lever down.

"She handed me a large container of vitamin C tablets and insisted you take them."

"Me? Interesting."

"Mol and I are going to go shopping today. I'll pick some up for you."

With his back toward me, Dad poured himself a cup of coffee. I persisted.

"Dad, she was quite insistent that you take them."

"You pick them up and I will take them. I promise."

*   *   *

After enjoying a big breakfast Sunday morning and packing our laundered clothes, Mol and I headed back to college mid-afternoon. We were returning to a week of classes before two weeks of scheduled exams prior to separating again for Christmas break.

I received a text while driving. Mol glanced at my phone on the console.

"It's Jasper. He wants to know when you will be back on campus."

I gave her my code to unlock my phone. "Tell him we will be there within an hour." I waited for her to reply.

"He said to text him when you drive up to the dorm. He will help us unload."

Mol replied. I assumed she agreed to his request.

"He's so nice." She returned my phone to the console.

True to his word, he was waiting for us in the lobby as we pulled up to the dorm.

"Hello, ladies. Did you have a good break?"

His particularly good mood brought a smile to my face.

"Yes, we ate a lot and did some shopping." I looked at Mol.

"I had no idea your Thanksgiving meal involved so much food."

After Jasper helped us carry everything from my car to our room, I pulled my car keys from the lock on our door.

"I'll be back. I've got to go park my car."

Jasper looked toward me. "I'll go with you." He extended his hand toward me. "I can drive."

I surrendered the keys. "How was your break?"

"Good, but I'm glad to be back." He winked at me before opening the passenger door for me to get in my car. A true gentleman, and such a flirt.

It was a short drive to the lot and a nice walk back to the dorm as the day's sky turned to dusk. Distracted by conversation, I nearly stepped into an intersection as a car careened around the corner. The driver failed to see that I had the right of way. Jasper stepped in front of me, spreading his arms wide, and pushed me backward as the car's bumper came within inches of his knee. The driver of the car accelerated and continued without hesitation. Jasper turned toward me and grasped my arm.

"Are you OK?" He was clearly shaken by the event.

"Yes." I looked at his face, a mask of concern. "Thanks for stepping in front of me. I think the crazy driver would have actually hit me."

"He didn't even bother to look." He stared at the fading tail lights and sighed. "Here, give me your hand." He took my hand within his, placing himself between me and the road before we continued toward the dorm, and we arrived safely.

*   *   *

Between working in the library and studying for exams, the next three weeks went by quickly. Even though Jasper had a quiet place to study in his room, he spent a lot of his time in our room studying with Mol and me.

After having dinner with us, Jasper returned to his room to study. He had one exam left to take the next day. Since he was alone, I thought this would be a good time to give him the Christmas present I had got him. With the small box wrapped in red Christmas paper topped with a green bow in my hand, I went to Jasper's room, knocked on his door, and waited. It didn't take long for him to open it.

"Hi, and what do I owe the pleasure of your unexpected visit, my lady?"

I smiled, chuckling as he motioned for me to enter his room.

"I just wanted to give you this small token of my appreciation for your gallantry. You always seem to be there when I need you most."

He stared at the gift. A twinge of guilt registered within his eyes. He looked at me, unsmiling. "But I didn't get you anything."

"It doesn't matter. It's more of a joke anyway." I extended the gift toward him. "Just open it."

He accepted the gift, unwrapped it, and raised the lid to see a tiny pewter knight with its sword held high and a shield displayed on the opposite arm.

"A knight?" He picked it up, rotating it to view it in its entirety.

"Yes, it reminded me of you. Merry Christmas."

"Thank you." He set the empty package and knight upon his desk, wrapped his arms around me, and gently pulled me against his chest. "Merry Christmas."

His embrace was tender, yet strong, secure, and made me feel safe as if being in his embrace was natural, my rightful place. I reciprocated his hug. He released me and looked down into my eyes.

"When are you leaving for home?"

"Tomorrow morning after I drop Mol at the bus station. She is traveling during Christmas break. How about you?"

"I still have one exam to take in the morning, so tomorrow afternoon. I'll call you during the break, OK?"

"OK."

"Thank you for my present and drive carefully tomorrow."

"I will. You too. Bye."

When I returned to my room, Mol and I exchanged Christmas presents. She gave me a Claddagh ring, explained its significance, and how to wear it. I gave her a warm set of gloves, hat, and scarf with our college logo on it. Afterward, I packed for my return home while she grilled me for information on Jasper's reaction to his gift.

"Well, did he like it?"

"I guess so. He gave me a hug and said he would call me over break."

She couldn't contain her smile.

"See, I told you he likes you. You two are destined to be together."

"I don't know. I mean, he's nice."

191

"Nice! Are you kidding me? Admit it. He is drop dead hot."

I sighed and gave her a grin. "Fine. He is pretty hot."

"Damn right. I'd be crawling into bed with him in a heartbeat."

I bet you would. I pulled my hamper from the closet, put my Christmas gifts for my family in a plastic bag, and set them next to the door with the other items I would take home with me during break.

*   *   *

After a quick breakfast and driving Mol to the bus station, I made my way home for Christmas break. I was glad to have finals behind me, be home with family, and return to my old job to replenish my checking account.

I put my bag in my bedroom and peeked into Dad's room. *I wonder...*I went to his closet and opened the door. Mom's clothes were still on the hangers. Her dresser drawers were still full too. I pulled open the bottom drawer and found the trinkets my brother and I had given her over the years. The silly art projects made in elementary school art class for Mother's Day must have meant a lot to her.

I decorated for the holiday knowing I would have to take down the decorations before I returned to college, so I didn't go too crazy and overdo it.

FROM BEYOND THE GRAVE

The tree was lit in all its splendor with presents beneath it, waiting to be opened on Christmas morning. Our stockings, made by Mom many years ago, hung on the fireplace mantel. I had not planned to stuff them, so I hoped Dad had taken it upon himself to do so. I would have to ask him once he arrived home from work. I baked several types of cookies and contacted Grandma to plan our Christmas dinner menu.

Our Bond Becomes Stronger

It was Christmas Eve. I took the frozen cookies from the freezer, an oval tray from the cupboard, and placed a variety of cookies upon it. The doorbell rang. *Can't be Grandma. She usually knocks then calls out as she enters without waiting for us to open the door.* I went to the door and answered it. A delivery man stood with a box.

"Elizabeth Michaels?"

"Yes."

"These are for you. Merry Christmas."

"Thank you. Merry Christmas to you as well." I accepted the long narrow white box with the large red bow and shut the door.

There was a little card tucked into the red ribbon. Setting the box on the table, I pulled the envelope from the ribbon, opened it, and read the card.

'Miss you. Merry Christmas! Jasper.'

I set the card on the counter, opened the box, and pulled aside the green waxy tissue paper to reveal beautiful, long-stemmed pale pink roses. I inhaled deeply. *Oh, they're so pretty.*

Dad walked into the kitchen.

"Who was at the door?"

I took a tall vase from the cupboard and filled it with water.

"A delivery man."

I retrieved a pair of scissors from the junk drawer, snipped the little packet that lay atop of the roses, and sprinkled it in the water. Dad peeked over my shoulder as I took one of the roses from the box.

"Oh, what do we have here?"

My brother walked into the kitchen.

"Who was at the door?" He watched as I snipped the rose and placed it in the vase. "Wow, those are nice. Who are they from?

"They're from Jasper." I picked up the card and read it again to verify how it was signed.

My brother scoffed.

"The same 'friend' who called you at Thanksgiving? I have a feeling that he's more than just a friend."

"We aren't going out if that's what you are implying."

My brother looked to Dad, Dad returned his all-knowing stare.

"Elizabeth, I think he intends to be more than 'just friends'." Dad made quotations marks in the air to emphasize his point before taking a cookie from the platter and leaving the room. I looked to my brother who was nodding in agreement with Dad's assessment before helping himself to several cookies and departing.

I continued to snip each rose and arrange it in the vase, along with the baby's breath as a garnish. Strange, a white feather lay in the bottom of the box as well. I picked it up and twirled it between my thumb and index finger. *Mom?*

With the bouquet finished, I placed it in the center of the kitchen table and stared at the beautiful arrangement, thinking. *Even Mol suspects Jasper's fondness for me.* I looked at the feather, still between my fingers, and back to the roses. Was it a coincidence the roses were the same color Mom had had on her casket?

I picked up my cell phone from the counter and called Jasper. He answered on the second ring.

"Hi, Elizabeth."

"Hi. I received a very nice delivery a few minutes ago."

"Oh, good. They arrived. The florist didn't know if they would have time to deliver them before Christmas."

"They're beautiful. Thank you."

"You're welcome. I wanted to get you something for Christmas and I know it seems a little clichéd, but it was the only thing I could think of to get you."

I guess the only way to find out his true feeling toward me is to ask him.

"There is something I need to ask you."

"What?"

"My Dad and my brother insinuated that the flowers have a deeper meaning."

"Such as?"

Oh, he's going to make me say it. Really?

"That you would like to pursue a relationship, with me, like, more than just a friendly relationship."

"Elizabeth, I'm quite fond of you and yes, I think our friendship is solid, rock solid, but it is also more than that, at least to me."

I didn't know what to say, so I remained silent. He continued.

"When we are together, it just somehow feels... right. Holding your hand, hugging you, having you in my arms. I'm not gonna lie, it feels pretty good. And let's face it, you need to have me close by, on guard, to keep you safe."

I laughed. *He has a point.* And not just about keeping me safe. The hug had been amazing.

"Elizabeth, I miss you and haven't stopped thinking about you since you left on break."

The conversation was getting a little deep. I wasn't ready to reveal my feelings. Feelings? Did I have feelings for him? I thought it best to change the subject.

"Hey, how did you know where to send the flowers?"

"Mol told me."

"Ah, I might have known Mol had a hand in this."

"Don't be mad at her. She only did as I asked."

"I'm not mad."

"Good. So, getting back to the conversation about us."

Great, he's being persistent.

"OK."

"How do you feel about dating, about giving us a go?"

I sighed. "Um, well, I've never been in a relationship before."

Silence.

"That's good to know, because neither have I."

Now I was silent. I thought all guys, at least most of the guys I knew, had had several girlfriends in high school, let alone college.

"Oh."

"So, you see, we're perfect for each other. Together we'll figure this relationship thing out, no matter how awkward it may get at times. Deal?"

I smiled. "Deal."

*   *   *

"So, they finally found each other." I sighed as I turned to my spirit guide.

"*Yes, their paths have crossed and become one. However, their individual paths remain.*"

"How so?"

"*They must learn individually as well.*"

"Ah, I see."

"*And it must be remembered, not all relationships are meant to be. For instance, many may experience a relationship in which they are to learn to walk away from it.*"

"Such as divorce?"

He simply nodded.

"But not this one, right?"

He did not reply.

*   *   *

Our family Christmas was the usual traditional celebration. Midnight Mass, a big breakfast, and then opening gifts. Dinner at Grandma's house went well until my brother mentioned the flowers from Jasper while we played a board game. Grandma insisted on pursuing as much information as I was willing to divulge about him.

"He's the one who called you the last time you were here, right?"

"Yes."

"So, he's an official boyfriend now?"

I cringed internally.

"I guess. We have agreed to 'officially' date." I used my fingers as quote marks.

"Do you think you're going to get married?"

Seriously, Grandma?

"I think it's a little premature to assume that." I rolled the dice and began counting out loud hoping she would drop the subject. While I waited for Grandma to take her turn, I sent a quick text telling Jasper I would call him after we arrived home. The last thing I needed was another interrogation after talking to my boyfriend.

Boyfriend. It was strange to think of Jasper as such. With us spending a lot of time together at college, his absence made me feel as if something was missing. Was it more of a habit to have him near me? Was I in love with him? In a way, yes. Were my feelings for him as strong as his feelings for me? I had yet to understand the depth of his affection or, for that matter, mine.

FROM BEYOND THE GRAVE

*   *   *

I woke the next morning to discover Spooky lying on the floor of my bedroom. I went to the kitchen, put his canned food in his dish, and noticed he had not followed me downstairs. I called him, waited, but he did not come. Returning to my bedroom, I found him standing on shaky legs, staring up at me. I picked him up, cuddled him as I went to the kitchen, and set him before his food. He ate, but shortly afterward I watched him lower himself to the floor as if every joint in his body hurt.

"You aren't doing so well today, are you Spook?"

I put a towel on the rug near the heater vent below the kitchen sink, and laid him on the towel hoping he would stay warm. He had so little body fat left.

I gathered the ingredients to bake some Christmas cookies and kept a watchful eye on his steady decline. As he began to lose his bodily functions, I changed the towel and laid him down once again.

"It's OK, Spooky." I stroked his fur as he lay his head down. I could feel every vertebra in his spine. My cookie dough could wait. Assuming his time was drawing near, I sat by his side, continued to speak softly, and pet him. I could feel his body becoming stiff, his breathing shallow. As he stopped breathing, his head bent backward nearly touching his spine. His legs stiffened before his back legs began kicking simultaneously, then the left leg by itself, then the right. His body finally stilled, and his head returned to its normal position. I leaned forward and pressed my ear to his chest. I could hear him purring. I sat up and looked to his chest. He still wasn't breathing. I listed once again. His purring faded. His heart beat several times before it became silent. I sat upright and stroked his fur one last time.

"Goodbye, Spooky." I wrapped his body in the towel, assuming he would be buried within it.

Once home from work, Dad dug a whole next to the house where the ground remained unfrozen. He placed Spooky's wrapped body inside and buried him.

I often found myself looking to the floor for Spooky, expecting him to brush up against my leg or staring at me to share with him something I was eating. I missed him and found myself tearing up at the mere thought or a memory of him.

Three nights later, I woke during the night. I could hear items on my dresser being moved around. *Spooky?* Was he letting me know he was still there, or that at least his spirit was still with me? I liked to believe he was letting me know that he was fine and free from pain.

Jasper and I decided he would come to my house on New Year's Eve to meet my family.

I was thankful to be scheduled to work for the next few days. It was good to keep my mind distracted. I grieved over the loss of our cat and was nervous about Jasper meeting my family. Hoping to ensure Dad was in a good mood, I planned to make lasagna for dinner that night, his favorite.

FROM BEYOND THE GRAVE

The day before Jasper arrived, I worked the morning shift. I stopped at the grocery store on my way home. It was strange not to have to buy cat food. Once home, I prepared a simple dinner of grilled cheese with tomato soup. During the meal, the chair my brother was sitting on broke. Dad glued it as best he could. Since there would be four of us for dinner tomorrow night and I weighed the least, I would sit on the repaired chair during the meal and pray it held together. Uneasy and hoping everything went well, I tossed and turned until the early morning hours before I fell asleep.

~

I was scanning the legs of a chair to ensure they were secure. When I got near the floor, Spooky was sitting beneath the chair. His little front paws were tucked under his chest. He looked healthy, so fluffy and chubby. He looked up at me.

"Meow."

I smiled, so surprised to see him there. Was he telling me that he was fine? Not to worry or grieve anymore?

~

At first morning's light, I jotted down the dream in my journal, ensured the house was thoroughly cleaned, and had the lasagna made and in the refrigerator. Jasper arrived after lunch and seemed quite at ease as he entered the house, took off his shoes, and looked my Dad in the eye as he shook his hand. My brother had decided to spend the day and evening with friends, so all the worrying I'd done about the repaired chair was unnecessary.

"Sir, could I have a moment of your time? I would like to ask you something."

I looked at Jasper and then to Dad. *What is going on*?

Dad motioned toward the living room / Mom's office. They spoke quietly so I could not overhear their conversation. Moments later Jasper rejoined me. He clapped his hands together, had a big smile on his face, and there seemed to be a spring in his step. I couldn't help but grin.

"You seem happy."

"I am." He clasped my hand within his, brought it to his lips, and kissed the back of it.

"Why?"

He pulled me into his arms, wrapping them around me gently.

"I asked your dad for his permission to date you and he said yes."

I looked up into his baby blue eyes. His devilish smile was contagious.

"You asked my dad?"

"I thought it would be appropriate. Anyways, it couldn't hurt unless he told me no."

I baked the lasagna, heated the green beans, and sliced the fresh bread from our local bakery. With everyone seated and the food on the table, we enjoyed a nice meal together. Dad and Jasper seemed to hit it off well. Their main topic of conversation was sports.

After clearing our plates, I served my favorite, gooey, chocolate frosted brownies. They were the perfect ending to a yummy meal.

Dad helped himself to a second brownie.

"Jasper, I expect you to spend the night."

My mouth dropped open as my head snapped toward my conservative father. *What was he implying*? I waited as he continued. "There are too many drunks out there after midnight, so you can stay here and sleep on the couch or, if you prefer, we have a blow-up mattress." Dad looked toward me as I closed my mouth, grinned, and looked at Jasper.

"Thank you. I only live an hour away from here, but may take you up on your offer if you don't mind."

"Don't mind at all." Dad ate a forkful of brownie.

Well, I guess that's settled.

After a quick clean-up of the kitchen, the three of us watched the impressive fireworks from each country as the holiday celebration made its way around the world. Dad adjourned to his bedroom a few hours before midnight and continued to watch TV. Jasper took the opportunity to put his

205

arm over my shoulders and grasp my hand. He looked toward my right hand and scowled.

"What's this?"

I looked down at my hand to see his thumb tracing my ring.

"Oh, that's my Christmas present from Mol. It's an Irish tradition. She said the way I'm wearing it with the point of the heart outward means I am single. If the point of the heart was inward, it means I'm not available. If it is on my left hand and outward, it means I am engaged, inward means I am married."

"I see. Well, we've some unfinished business to attend to." He slipped the Claddagh ring from my finger and replaced it with the point of the heart inward. "You know, the first day I met you, I fell in love with you. I knew that you were the one for me, but I also knew you didn't feel the same. After bumping into you, you know the night you were upset, I thought it best to take things slow, to earn your trust. Do you know what I learned?"

I shook my head. "No."

"The more time we've spent together, the more it has affirmed what is within my heart to be true. I feel at ease, a comfort between us as if we were meant to be. I'm here for you and you are here for me."

I smiled. "I couldn't have said it any better. You've described us perfectly."

We remained cuddled on the couch and watched the ball drop. Jasper lifted my chin and he leaned toward me.

"Happy New Year."

I smiled. "Happy New Year."

"May I kiss you?"

"I believe it's a tradition. So, you kind of have to."

*   *   *

The TV was on low with the screen illuminating the bedroom. My husband snored, missing the ball drop.

"I remember when we watched the ball drop together. It's sad he is spending the new year alone."

"*He has the children with him.*"

"You know what I mean. It's a tradition to celebrate the new year, kiss someone at the stroke of midnight."

"*You will once again do so, with him, and soon.*"

I looked to his spirit guide, who nodded his head knowing I understood his implication.

Back from Break

Mol was waiting for me when I arrived. She bubbled with excitement while I unpacked.

"New York was amazing. Have you ever been there for New Year's Eve?"

"No, but how did you find a place to stay?"

"It was easy. I stayed in a hostel. They're inexpensive."

"Sounds a little creepy to me."

"The bus was quite accommodating, and I was able to see a lot. I wouldn't be able to manage driving on the opposite side of the road and…"

"Hello, ladies." Jasper strolled through our open doorway.

Distracted, Mol paused and looked toward the door.

"Hi, Jasper. I was just telling Elizabeth about my adventures in New York."

"Hold that thought, Mol." He clasped my hand within his, guided me into the hallway, and backed me against the wall. He wove his hand around my waist and leaned towards me.

"I missed you." He smiled.

"I missed you too."

He leaned down and touched his lips gently to mine before brushing a kiss on my forehead.

"I've been thinking about doing that ever since New Year's Eve."

"I must admit, you do know how to take advantage of me once you have me pinned against the wall." I chuckled.

"Well, since you are in such a compromising position, I'll just take the opportunity once again." He spread his legs wide to lower his height until his face was level with mine, cupped my face with his right hand and pulled me toward him as he kissed me. Almost instinctively, I wrapped my arms around him and deepened our kiss.

A door slammed, startling us both. We broke off the kiss and looked in the direction of the noise.

Jasper stood tall, wrapped his arms around me and lifted me off the floor. He couldn't contain his happiness.

I smiled. "We better go listen to Mol's tales before she comes looking for us."

We went back into the room. Mol had this all-knowing look upon her face. "Well, it's about time you two hooked up."

We both laughed as I looked at Mol. Jasper stepped behind me and wrapped his arms around my waist. I looked down at his entwined fingers on my stomach and focused on a tiny white feather on the floor by my feet. I smiled. *Thanks, Mom. Apparently, you approve of him too.*

Until We Meet Again

An afterlife journey ~ Part 3

Brenda Hasse

Available 2020

Continuing Onward

My first year of college ended with a farewell to my Irish roommate, Mol. After shipping most of her non-essential items home and overstuffing her backpack, Jasper and I drove her to the bus stop.

He pulled his car alongside the curb and put it into park. Together, we walked Mol to the door. I sighed as I turned toward my foreign friend.

"Text me often and let me know that you are safe."

Mol embraced me. "I promise, I will. I'm quite excited to see the rest of the country."

"You'll be staying in hostels the entire time?" I always thought traveling by bus and staying in rent-a-bed, communal hostels was risky and a little scary. After all, one never knows who they will be sharing a room with, possibly someone of the opposite sex.

"Wouldn't have it any other way." Mol turned to Jasper. "Take care of my roomy."

She reached upward to wrap her arms around his broad shoulders. He bent down and enveloped her small body with his arms.

"Absolutely. You take care now. Keep in touch and call if you need anything."

"Shall do. Bye." Mol squeezed my arm as she passed by me, opened the door to the bus station, and began her adventure. As promised, she kept in touch via text and the internet and shared her adventure with us until she caught a flight home.

Home for the summer, I returned to the job I had retained for the past few years, managed to take two online courses, and keep Mom's flower garden in order. Dad seemed different, quiet, as we watched a movie together one evening. He left to the room and returned with a few moments. It was the third time he had used the bathroom within the hour. I stared at him as he sat in his recliner chair and put his feet up.

"Dad, what's going on? You don't seem like yourself."

"Nothing to worry about. Just having trouble urinating, but I've seen a doctor."

A doctor? Dad never went to the doctor for any ailment.

"When did you begin having trouble?"

"First of the year, but like I said, the doctor is monitoring the issue. He recently increased my medication."

Increased medication? A twinge of panic tightened my stomach. *Was or wasn't the medication working*? I kept the thought to myself.

I saw Jasper as often as our schedules would allow. My relationship with him was pleasantly surprising. I'd heard of other couples having arguments or all out 'fights'. Jasper and I were more like best friends who never argued. I wondered if others thought our relationship to be strange.

As my summer was ending and I prepared to return to college, I arrived home from work one afternoon to find Dad sitting at the kitchen table. He looked up from the paperwork he was reading.

"Hi. Why are you home? Did you have the day off from work?"

"Yes, I had a follow-up with my doctor. He is recommending I see an oncologist."

My heart skipped a beat. "Oncologist?" I had to think for a moment. I sat down at the table. "You mean a cancer doctor?"

"Yes. My doctor suspects I have prostate cancer."

"So, it's not confirmed?"

"He's quite certain he is correct."

I wanted to cry, but I was too shocked to do so. Was Dad going to die?

Dad reached across the table and patted my hand as if reading my mind.

"Most men don't die from prostate cancer. It's a slow growing cancer, but I won't know the extent of it until I see the oncologist. He or she will probably order a CT scan and do some further testing. Let's not jump to conclusions and take this one step at a time, OK?"

I tried to smile as I nodded in agreement.

I hope you enjoyed reading

From Beyond The Grave.

If so, your review on Amazon.com

would be greatly appreciated.

For further information about

Brenda Hasse Books,

please visit

www.BrendaHasseBooks.com.

9 780990 631279